SWALLOWCLIFFE HALL

HOUSE OF
SECRETS

SWALLOWCLIFFE HALL

HOUSE OF
SECRETS

JENNIE WALTERS

SIMON AND SCHUSTER

First published in Great Britain by Simon & Schuster UK Ltd, 2005
A Viacom company

www.swallowcliffe hall.com

1 3 5 7 9 10 8 6 4 2

Simon & Schuster UK Ltd
Africa House
64-78 Kingsway
London WC2B 6AH

A CIP catalogue record for this book is available from the British Library

ISBN 0 689 87526 6

Typeset by SX Composing DTP, Rayleigh, Essex
Printed by Cox & Wyman, Reading, Berkshire

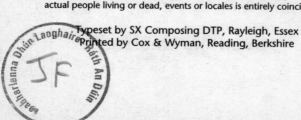

For Harriet Stallibrass

ONE

A good constitution and a willing disposition are amongst the principal qualities to seek in a housemaid, to which may be added a quiet, pleasing manner and cleanly appearance . . . A housemaid's dress is of some importance. When engaged in her morning work, washable materials are the best; a wide holland apron should always be worn over one of white material whenever house-cleaning is going on. Thick boots, especially with nails, are destructive to stair carpets, and should on no account be worn in the house.

From *Cassell's Household Guide*, c. 1880s

I stood on the doorstep of the big house, my heart thumping so hard it was fit to jump out of my chest, raised the knocker and brought it down with a clap that echoed around the empty courtyard. A couple of pigeons pecking at crumbs on the cobblestones fluttered up into the air; such a great noise in that quiet place startled me, too, even though I had made it myself. For two pins I would have taken up my basket and run all the way home, but there could be no turning back: the new year had begun and with it, a new life for me. I had arrived to start work as under housemaid at Swallowcliffe Hall – if only someone would let me in.

I wished now that I had come by train and let the coachman meet me at the station, as the housekeeper had suggested when I came for my interview a couple of weeks before. That had seemed a great deal of fuss at the time, however, so my mother and I had decided to beg a lift halfway on the dairy cart, and walk the rest. It was a frosty January morning but we were wrapped up against the cold, and tramping along the country lanes helped keep us warm. I wanted to put off the moment when we had to part for as long as possible, and maybe my mother felt the same. We have always been close, especially since my father died, and I could not bear the thought of leaving her.

'Now chin up, Polly,' she had told me as we stood together by the tall iron gates at the top of the drive. 'You're as good as anyone else, and better than most. Work hard and remember your manners, and no one will have any cause for complaint.'

Then she pressed a small paper package into my hand, telling me to open it later, and hugged me tight. A boy came out of the lodge to open the side gate and let me through; by the time I looked again, my mother was walking away down the long avenue of oak trees on either side of the road. The gate clanged shut, with me on one side and everything I knew and loved on the other. I had to bite my tongue not to call after her, feeling as though I had been abandoned in some strange foreign country to fend for myself as best I could. But then I noticed the gatekeeper's boy staring at me – probably wondering how much longer I planned to stand there, moping like a mooncalf – so I took Mother's words to heart, straightened my shoulders and set off up the drive with as much courage as I could muster.

Fancy me, becoming part of a gentleman's household! There have been Vyes at Swallowcliffe for hundreds of years, and the present Lord Vye was talked about with a great deal of respect throughout the whole of Kent. I could hardly believe my luck when the housekeeper told me she would take me on – at fourteen pounds a year, which worked out at three pounds ten shillings per quarter! I would be on a month's trial, mind, since I was only fourteen and she did not know whether I would be able to manage the work. If I had not been tall for my age and with such a good character reference from my previous employers, Reverend Conway and his daughter, I'm sure she would never have considered it. I had read Miss

Conway's letter so many times, I knew it off by heart:

> *Olive Perkins has been employed as a general*
> *servant at the vicarage for the past eighteen months,*
> *and my father and I can vouch for her as a steady,*
> *industrious girl of good character. She has a quiet,*
> *pleasant manner and comes from a respectable*
> *church-going family who have fallen on hard times*
> *through no fault of their own. Olive does not mind*
> *heavy work; she is healthy and strong for her years.*
> *She knows how to clean and polish thoroughly and*
> *is skilled at needlework, both plain and fancy.*

Olive was the name I had been christened with, although everyone has called me Polly since I was a baby. I suppose Miss Conway thought that Polly Perkins did not sound a sufficiently serious kind of person to be employed at Swallowcliffe, and that Olive would be more suitable.

Being the oldest of four children, it was taken for granted that I would start earning my living as soon as possible to help provide for the family. I had begun by scrubbing floors and backyards on a Saturday for any of our neighbours who could spare the odd penny or a slice of bread, and that is how I came to know Miss Conway. She took a liking to me, which was a great stroke of luck after all the sad things that had happened to us; my mother also having lost the baby she was carrying shortly after my father died. He was a fisherman, and had been drowned in a storm at sea when I was ten. This marked the start of hard times for our family. There had been hardly enough for the five of us to live on ever since and besides, we all missed him a great deal – even my little brother, who was only a baby at the time. Eventually, upon leaving school I came to the vicarage as a maid-of-all-work. The Conways could only afford to pay me eight pounds a year, but I took my meals with Miss Conway – although it has to be said that she ate no more than a sparrow and assumed I would do the same. She trained me in all sorts of household duties, from blackleading the kitchen range to sweeping a carpet with damp tea leaves so the dust won't fly about, plus everything you could possibly want to know about dusting, polishing and making beds, and a lot more besides. I learned a great deal and managed to save enough to buy a black uniform dress ready for my next position. Then, as if by fate, my mother heard that they were looking for a housemaid at the Hall; the girl who was leaving happened to be a niece of one of our neighbours. News travels fast in a village like Little Rising, with the cottages clustered so close together and somebody usually hanging over their garden fence for a gossip.

I think Miss Conway was sorry to see me go, since I was a hard worker and we had rubbed along together very well. She gave me a leather-bound prayer book on my last day at the vicarage, and a print frock, which I was wearing that morning. 'It will look better on you than an old maid like me,' she had said. Privately, I couldn't help but agree – Miss Conway not being overly blessed in the looks department, despite having all sorts of other virtues. Without wishing to sound vain, I thought the dress suited me very well. It was made from a crimson cotton and had a full skirt with several frilled petticoats underneath and wide flounced sleeves. Although it was a little too big for me around the waist, I am handy with a needle and soon had it altered to fit almost perfectly.

I might have felt quite pleased with myself in our little cottage, with the neighbours so jealous of my good luck and my younger sisters and brother telling me how fine I looked, but now I had arrived at the Hall, all the courage I possessed seemed to drain out through my boots. I will try to describe the place as best I can, though you would have to see Swallowcliffe for yourself to understand its magic. The main house is three storeys high, built from a honey-coloured stone which weathers to a silvery-grey in places over time. There is a grey slate roof with dormer windows set into it, a parapet around the edge and a little round tower in the middle which I think is called a cupola. On top of that is the weather vane: a golden swallow who swings about as the wind takes him, looking out over the formal gardens and the lake to the south of the house, or

6

the winding drive and avenue of oak trees to the north, or east and west across miles of rolling parkland to the wooded hills that rise up behind.

I had not come to the Hall's main entrance: two long flights of steps leading up to a huge door. That was not for the likes of me. Instead, I had taken a back path to reach the servants' wing, which was laid out around a courtyard at the west side of the house. I could remember coming this way with my mother on our previous visit, but that had been later in the day when there were more people about to show us where to go next. I rubbed my frozen hands together to bring some feeling back into them and wondered what to do; Mrs Henderson, the housekeeper, was expecting me and soon I would be late. Plucking up courage, I knocked again. Still no answer.

Come on, Polly, I told myself sternly, do you plan to dither about on this step the whole morning long? There was nothing for it but to let myself in, whatever the consequences. I picked up my basket, tried the door to see if it was locked, then swung it open and walked down the passage on the other side. So far, so good – except for the fact that I could not recognise any familiar features and did not have the faintest idea how to find my way to the housekeeper's room. Still, I would probably soon come across someone who could direct me; a faint clattering (pots and pans, maybe) and distant voices further down the corridor told me I was heading in the right direction.

After a couple of interesting excursions into some sort of pantry and a boot room (both deserted, thank goodness), I opened another door in the passage and half-stumbled, half-fell down a shallow step into the largest kitchen I had ever seen. A rush of hot air hit me in the face, rich with the delicious smells of frying bacon, freshly-baked bread, toast and coffee. Steam rose up from saucepans bubbling away on the huge black range, and there were more gleaming copper pans hanging on the wall opposite. Three or four kitchenmaids were hard at work: one slicing bread, another whirling round the handle of an egg whisk as if her life depended on it, another heaping kippers on to a silver salver. Standing at the vast oak table in the middle of the room was a red-faced, broad-shouldered woman with a knife in one hand, whom I took to be the cook. She stared at me in astonishment.

'Well, this is an unexpected pleasure!' she shouted above the hustle and bustle, upon which the girls all stopped what they were doing to stare at me too. 'Who might you be, young lady?'

'I'm the new housemaid, ma'am,' I said, trying to pick up my basket and curtsey at the same time.

'Then what are you doing here?' she interrupted, before I could say any more. 'Some sort of halfwit, are you? Take a look around and tell me where you think this is.'

'The kitchen, ma'am,' I began, noticing that the girls had started smiling at me and whispering amongst themselves in a rather unpleasant way, 'but I don't know—'

'Yes, the kitchen!' she boomed. 'And we are in the middle of preparing breakfast. So, out! Get out, right this minute and don't come bothering us again if you know what's good for you.' And she made as if to throw the knife at my head!

Well! I took up my basket pretty sharpish and out I went, my face burning and all sorts of feelings welling up inside me. Now I was embarrassed and ashamed, as well as nervous – and quite indignant, too. There was no call to speak to me like that! The more I thought about it, the angrier I became, until I found myself marching down the corridor in a proper temper (and still with no idea whatsoever as to where I should be going).

'Steady on! Where are you off to in such a hurry?'

I found myself glaring up at a tall young man in a dark uniform with brass buttons, carrying a silver tray. I had walked straight into one of the footmen, though I was far too cross to think about apologising. 'I am the new housemaid,' I said again, my voice rising, 'and I am trying to find the housekeeper's room and no one will tell me where it is!'

'Well, I will. It is not a secret,' he said, beginning to smile. 'In fact, I can take you there if you like.'

All of a sudden, the anger went straight out of me. 'I am sorry,' I said, feeling as though I could sit down right there and then and burst into tears. 'I went into the kitchen by mistake and the cook went to throw a knife at me.'

'Ah, so you have met Mrs Bragg,' he said, smiling even more broadly. 'There is no need to worry yourself about her. She is a very bad shot. That is why all those pans are hanging on the wall, you see: target practice. She hasn't managed to hit one yet.'

I could not help but laugh at this, even though I was having to sniff quite hard at the same time so as not to cry. The young man kindly lent me a handkerchief and waited for a few moments whilst I composed myself, and then we went off to find the housekeeper's room. I could hardly believe myself, walking along the corridor bold as brass with a footman – powdered hair, smart livery and all! (Even though he was being so friendly and obliging.) He told me his name was William, and I told him my name was Polly, and then we were at Mrs Henderson's door and he had gone away before I could properly thank him. I took a couple of deep breaths to steady my nerves, knocked on the door and waited to be admitted.

Mrs Henderson was sitting behind her desk, dressed all in black with a bunch of keys hanging at her waist, and just as fearsome as I remembered from my interview: ramrod straight and dignified, with pale, watery eyes and iron grey hair scraped back under her cap. After looking me up and down for a few moments without speaking, at last she said in a brisk, clipped sort of voice – and I can hardly bear to recall her words, even now – 'Whatever have you got yourself dressed up in, girl? You can't go about like something out of the circus! Do you not have anything more suitable to wear?'

At first I could only stand there, gawping at her like a fish. Could she really be talking about my wonderful frock? I stared down at it, smoothing the fabric, then back into Mrs Henderson's cold eyes. And all of a sudden, I saw myself reflected there as she must have seen me – a silly young girl in a garish outfit that had probably only ever been fashionable years ago – and blushed to the roots of my hair. To have gone so wrong before I even started work! It was awful.

'I have my black uniform dress,' I stammered, 'only I should not like to get it dirty.' This was the only other frock I possessed, having given the old blue serge to my younger sister, Lizzie, on leaving home. It was far too short for me now, anyway.

'Oh, never mind,' Mrs Henderson muttered. 'I suppose that will have to do for this morning, with a decent apron over it. We can find you something else by tomorrow. When is your box arriving?'

I had no box; everything I owned in the world was in

that wicker basket. But I did not want to admit this to the housekeeper and have her thinking I was one step away from the workhouse, so I told her it would be arriving by train later on in the week. With any luck, she would forget about it.

Mrs Henderson nodded and reached up to ring a bell on the wall by the side of her desk. 'Mary is the head housemaid here. She will show you up to your room and you can put away your things. Servants' breakfast is at eight o'clock prompt, and as the most junior housemaid you will wait on the others and help clear the table. After household prayers you will clean the female servants' quarters, and then work with the other maids in the family bedrooms . . .'

She rattled through my duties while I tried desperately to keep up. My head was soon spinning with so many instructions that I despaired of ever being able to remember them all, but I was presented with a written work timetable to keep in my apron pocket, together with two frilled caps. Then Mary appeared – tall and thin, with a harassed expression and the habit of chewing her lip – to hurry me off down another long corridor and up twisting flights of stairs. I followed behind her, trying to take note of every turn we took so that I would not get lost on the way back down.

'You will share a washstand and have two drawers of the chest for yourself,' Mary told me, all out of breath as she threw open the door to the attic room in which I was to sleep. 'That is your bed, over by the window. What have you brought with you?'

'My black uniform dress and two aprons,' I said. 'And black button boots for indoors.' They were my mother's best pair; goodness only knew how she would manage without them. 'Mrs Henderson gave me my caps.'

'Your hair needs some attention too,' Mary said, looking critically at me. 'Now put your things away, make your bed, and I'll see you downstairs in the servants' hall in ten minutes. Look lively, girl, for heaven's sake! There's plenty to be done.'

After I had made my bed, I sat down on it for a moment and looked around. It was a large room, rather dark and dreary, with a strip of threadbare carpet running along one side of the floor in front of the two heavy chests of drawers. The rest of the furniture consisted of a couple of washstands with china bowls sitting on them and four iron bedsteads with a wooden chair next to each one. I could see a fireplace, but it did not seem much used; there was no coal scuttle next to it and no sign of any ashes. Draughts rose up from the loose-fitting floorboards which creaked under my feet, and the window rattled in its frame when the wind blew hard outside. We had a lovely view, though: out across the lake to a patchwork of fields and hedgerows beyond. I knew that Lord Vye owned a great stretch of land in this corner of Kent, right down to the coast about fifteen miles away. Screwing up my eyes, I tried to catch a glimpse of the sea, but the only sign of it was a stray gull that had been blown inland, wheeling above the trees and calling out in the melancholy way those birds have.

A small mirror hung on the wall above the washstand, so I went over to brush my hair and pin it back up, with one of the caps perched on top. Mother always says my hair is my best feature: there is plenty of it, at least! But it is an unremarkable brown, as are my eyes; my complexion only has to see the sun to turn brown too, unfortunately. I have always been tall for my age, with long arms and legs and a strong back – just as well, when it comes to making beds. And that is all I can think of to say about my appearance; except that our neighbour, Mrs Grimshaw, once told my mother (in front of me) that her big ugly duckling looked like turning into a swan. I did not know quite what to make of this but, as Mother said, Mrs Grimshaw is so old and short-sighted there was no point in taking offence.

I looked at the three other beds and wondered about the girls who would be sharing the room with me that night. Would I find a friend among them? Despite my resolution to make the best of things, I couldn't help feeling that my new life had not got off to a very promising start.

TWO

Always move quietly about the house, and do not let your voice be heard by the family unless necessary. Never sing or whistle at your work where the family would be likely to hear you.

Do not call out from one room to another; and if you are a housemaid, be careful not only to do your work quietly, but to keep out of sight as much as possible.

From *A Few Rules for the Manners of Servants in Good Families*, 1901

I managed not to lose myself on the way back down to the servants' hall and was standing next to Mary by the time the gong sounded for breakfast, ready to hand around cups of tea and plates of cold ham which the under butler was waiting to carve. What a great number of people came rushing in to take their places at the long, scrubbed table! Thank goodness the upper servants were being provided with a separate meal in Mrs Henderson's room; it was enough for me to deal with the other maids and the footmen, so tall and grand in their tailcoats. I caught sight of William but did not feel able to say hello to him, as all the menservants were sitting on the opposite side of the table to the maids and there did not seem to be much conversation between the two parties. (Perhaps it was frowned upon; I did not yet know.) When I handed him his tea, however, he winked at me in a very encouraging way, which raised my spirits no end.

At last, everyone had been served and I could take my place at the end of the table, next to a pretty girl with dark curly hair and grey eyes. 'So you are the new housemaid,' she said, looking me up and down. 'How do you do? My name is Jemima Newgate, and Mary has paired me with you, for my sins. We shall be cleaning the servants' quarters together.' She gave me another cool glance. 'I hope you are prepared to do some work today, despite those fancy clothes.'

This remark did not exactly fill me with confidence, as you can imagine; in fact, I was not quite sure how to reply. 'I am quite used to hard work,' I said, stumbling over the words. 'My name is Polly, or Olive. It's nice to meet you. I'm sure we shall get along.'

'Are you, Polly or Olive?' she said, and laughed in a way which made me feel even more uncomfortable. 'Well, that

16

is good to know. You'd better be a quick learner, is all I can say, or we really shall be in trouble. Working with somebody new always takes twice as long.'

'Oh, Jemima! Don't be so contrary.' A fair-haired girl had just hurried into the servants' hall and taken the seat on Jemima's other side. She leaned forward to smile at me. 'You are quite right – we are all going to get along together very well indeed. My name is Iris. You will not have so much to do with me, because I am the still room maid, but we shall be sharing a room together. You, Jemima, myself and Becky,' and she pointed out another girl sitting further down the table. 'You cannot possibly snore as loudly as the poor creature who had your bed before, so we are all very pleased to see you.'

I smiled back and went to fetch her a cup of tea; at least there was one person who seemed to know how I felt and wanted to put me at my ease. Sadly, breakfast with Iris was over all too soon and then it was time for my next ordeal: prayers for the whole household in the chapel. The upper servants reappeared and we lined up in order of importance behind the butler (Mr Goddard was his name, I discovered later), who led the way along the passage and through the green baize-covered door, into the front of the house. This was the first time I had been beyond the servants' quarters, and I could hardly believe my eyes. It was like stepping through into another world. On one side

17

were bare wooden floorboards and rough plaster walls; on the other, acres of smooth marble and thick rugs underfoot. There were marble statues staring down at me from alcoves all along the hall, and a painted ceiling soared up high above my head. I had thought that the vicarage was very grand when I started working there, but you could have fitted the whole of that house into one little corner of the Hall without falling over it.

The chapel made me feel even more of a timid country mouse. It was such a solemn, quiet place, with the light falling softly through tall stained-glass windows and pictures of poor suffering saints and martyrs everywhere you looked. How Miss Conway would have loved it! Not a particularly large room but twice normal height, with a gallery upstairs for the family so they could look down on the pews where we sat. I couldn't resist taking a peek at the Vyes, whom I had not yet seen. The present Lord Vye had five children; four with his first wife (who had died after giving birth to their last daughter) and one son from his second marriage. The two older boys, Master Edward and Master Rory, were young men now and living away from home, so the only children at the Hall were the two daughters, Miss Eugenie and Miss Harriet, and their little half-brother, Master John, who was seven. I did not dare glance up at the gallery during prayers, but when I could tell from the noise of chairs being scraped back that the family was about to leave, I threw caution to the wind and took a quick peep.

There was His Lordship, looking exactly as I expected: very grave and serious. His dark hair and sidewhiskers were streaked with grey, but he was handsome and distinguished all the same, in a black frock coat and snowy white shirt. Lady Vye was a good deal younger. You wouldn't call her beautiful, exactly – her nose was a little too long and her eyes a little too heavy-lidded for that – but there was something about her face that made you want to gaze at it for a good long time. And the way she carried herself! As proud and regal as the Queen herself, in an elegant pearl-grey cashmere gown trimmed with lace, nipped in tight at the waist. I couldn't help admiring her quite openly. And then, to my dismay, she happened to notice me looking, and shot me such a furious stare in return that I could have died on the spot from the shame of it. I dropped my eyes immediately, with cheeks no doubt as red as my dress.

'You won't have been in a place like this before, I should imagine,' Jemima said with some satisfaction, as we hurried along to the housemaids' pantry after prayers to collect our cleaning boxes. 'And it all takes a lot of looking after, let me tell you that. Lord Vye isn't so bad – he only cares about his gardens, his dogs and his horses – but Her Ladyship is *very* particular. Everything has to be just so, or she'll put the fear of God into Mrs Henderson and then we get it in the neck. She never speaks directly to us, of course. And if she should ever pass you by, drop a curtsey with your eyes lowered. She doesn't appreciate being looked at by the likes of us. Ha! A cat may look at a queen, is what *I* say. Lady Vye isn't so special as that, for all her airs and graces.'

So that was the second mistake I had made, and not so much as a floor swept or a fire laid. If things did not look up, my first day at Swallowcliffe would end up being my last. I made up my mind to work as hard as ever I could, but Jemima's eyes were on me the whole morning long, and she seemed determined to find fault. She condescended to help me make the beds, but apart from that she spent most of the time watching me critically with her arms folded. Can you imagine anything more likely to make a person feel awkward and nervous? I had started off wanting to do my best, but she did not appear interested in teaching me how things should be done, which of course made everything take twice as long. And the more she chivvied me for being clumsy, the clumsier I became. Things improved a little when we joined up with the other housemaids to tidy the family's bedrooms, but then by chance I noticed that Jemima had swept a large cinder that was still alight into her workbox. (I nearly started a fire myself that way once, and have been particularly careful ever since.) I tried to point it out to her as quietly as I could, but unfortunately Mary overheard and told Jemima to be more careful – and she did *not* thank me for that, as you can imagine.

By the time we stopped work at one for our dinner, I felt in need of some friendly company, and was glad to stand beside Iris as we waited for the upper servants to take their places at the top of the table. What a feast was laid out for us! We had chicken and most of a huge turkey left over from upstairs which Mr Goddard carved, with Mrs Henderson dishing up potatoes, carrots and turnips picked from the kitchen garden. There was bread sauce, gravy and cranberry jelly on the table. I took around the plates with Barbara the scullerymaid, faint with hunger, and then finally sat down to enjoy my own meal. Jemima had moved up to sit next to Becky, so I was more than happy to take my place next to Iris.

'I've never seen such a quantity of food,' I remarked to her. 'Is there always so much to eat at midday? We shall be good for nothing this afternoon!'

She did not answer, but gave me a little shake of her head and a frown. Whatever was the matter? Could I possibly have offended her now? I was about to ask when I happened to glance up and saw to my horror that every single person down the length of that great long table was staring in my direction – including Mrs Henderson.

'Who is talking?' she demanded. 'Is that you, Olive?

Kindly refrain from speaking unless you are addressed by myself or Mr Goddard.'

Oh Lord, I had gone wrong again. 'Yes, ma'am,' I mumbled, dropping my eyes. How could I not have noticed that the lower end of the table was sitting in silence? A few seconds ago I could have polished off the whole turkey by myself; now I had suddenly lost my appetite. The food seemed to stick in my throat and I had to swallow hard to get down a single mouthful. Everybody must be thinking me such a fool! At last Mr Goddard finished eating and laid down his knife and fork; this was a signal for everybody else to do the same. I had to leave half the meal on my plate, which seemed a terrible waste. And then the upper servants went off to take their pudding and cheese in the housekeeper's room, leaving the rest of us to let out our breath and be sociable. Sadly for me, Iris went with them to wait at table. I was left with an empty place next to me and the feeling that I had been deserted by my one and only friend.

'Well, you *are* a bold one,' Jemima said to me at once, her eyes sparkling with mischief. 'Chatting merrily away in front of the upper servants, and on your first day too! We shall have to watch you.'

'I did not realise it was forbidden,' I replied. 'I shall know better another time.'

William was sitting opposite us, taking all this in, and

now he decided to join in the conversation. 'And what about *your* first day here, Jemima?' he asked, innocent as you please.

She stared at him for a moment and then glanced quickly away, as though he hadn't spoken. People were beginning to smile around us. 'Whose seat was it you took at the table?' William asked, as if wondering aloud to himself. 'I can't quite remember.'

'Then I'll thank you to keep your thoughts to yourself,' Jemima snapped – but too late.

'It was Lady Vye's maid,' called down one of the senior footmen, amid a general ripple of amusement. 'That French ma'm'selle with the hot temper. We thought she would crack you over the head with it!'

There was a burst of laughter at this, and now it was Jemima's turn to blush. She turned her back and began talking to Becky again. William winked at me. I did my best to smile back and thank him, though I knew he had landed me in yet more trouble and was worried about the consequences. Jemima would not take kindly to being shown up twice in one day.

In the afternoon, we housemaids had some sewing to do in our sitting room. It was so nice and peaceful, working away with only the sounds of a clock ticking on the mantelpiece and thread being drawn tight to disturb the quiet. I snatched the odd anxious glance at Jemima, but she had apparently decided to ignore me. Becky did not seem interested in talking to me either; I suppose that because she was Jemima's particular friend, she did not need to trouble herself with me. Mrs Henderson was busy with Iris in the still room, and came in every now and again to check on us. I was hemming a duster, as I remember (which had probably been judged not to matter very much and therefore suitable for the new girl), and she took it to the window to look at my stitching. When the cloth was returned to me with a nod, I couldn't have felt prouder than if Queen Victoria herself had presented me with a medal. At last there was something I could do properly!

'So, what are we to call you?' Mary asked me a little while later. 'Is it to be Polly or Olive? We must settle on something.'

'I was christened Olive, but Polly is how everyone knows me at home,' I replied, 'though it really doesn't matter. I'm not particular.'

'Then *I* shall call you Olive,' Jemima said suddenly, biting off a thread with one snap of her sharp, white teeth. 'It is such a dreary, drab sort of name – like that of some dull brown animal. A cow, perhaps, or a carthorse. I think it suits you very well.'

It took me a few seconds to understand the meaning of

her words. Why would anyone be so unpleasant to a person she had only just met? I stared at Jemima blankly, and the malice in her eyes made my own prickle with tears. Maybe I should have laughed to show I didn't care what she thought of me, or made some clever reply in return, but I was too shocked by her spiteful words to hide my feelings.

'Jemima!' Mary exclaimed. 'Whatever do you mean?'

'Oh, Olive doesn't mind me,' Jemima said. 'She knows I'm only teasing.' And she smiled at me as sweetly as if we were sisters. I realised she was happy because she had succeeded in upsetting me, and that hurt as much as the cruel thing she had said. I went back to my sewing with a heavy heart. All the pleasure had gone out of it now, and my stitches straggled higgledy-piggledy over the cloth.

For the rest of that day, I managed as best I could with my duties. There were fires to be lit in the bedrooms so that they would be warm when it was time to dress for dinner, hot water to be carried upstairs, and beds to be turned down when the family were installed in the dining room. Jemima and I hardly spoke to each other. I could not wait for the night to come, for the moment when I might pull the blanket over my head and have some time to myself. By the time our work was finally finished, I could hardly summon up the energy to take off my clothes, and lay down fully dressed on the bed. Jemima had already settled herself in the bed next to mine and was whispering with Becky, her back turned firmly away from me. My only consolation was the fact that Mrs Henderson had found me an old print dress to wear the next day which a previous housemaid had left behind. A shilling would be deducted from my first month's wages to pay for it – if I lasted that long, she added darkly.

And then, settling the lumpy pillow more comfortably, my hand came across the envelope Mother had given me that morning – so many lifetimes ago, it seemed. I had pushed it under the pillow to wait until later. Sitting up, I tore open the paper, and out fell a silver locket on a chain. There was a note with it.

> *For my dearest Polly,*
> *You will always be here in my heart, no matter how*
> *far you are from home. Wear this and remember*
> *how proud I am of you, and that your father is*
> *watching over us both in heaven.*
> *Your loving*
> *Mother*

I knew this locket well. It was the only piece of jewellery my mother had left, everything else (including her wedding ring) having been pawned since Father died. He had given her this necklace when they were courting, and now she had passed the precious gift on to me.

You might have thought that knowing there was someone in the world who loved me so dearly would have lifted my spirits, but the pillow was wet with tears by the time I eventually fell asleep. How could I ever make a life for myself in this strange, difficult place? I had never felt so completely alone in all my life.

THREE

Recollect, my little general servant, that if your place is a hard one, it is also the best possible one for training you for a better . . . If you rise early, bustle about, and waste no spare moments, you will get through your work very well. Only do think about it. A little arrangement and thought will give you Method and Habit, two fairies that will make the work disappear before a ready pair of hands.

From *Warne's Model Cookery*, c. 1890

'Polly, wake up!' For a moment I had no idea where I was – perhaps in the bed I shared at home with my younger sister Lizzie, who must have been telling me it was time to be up and off to the vicarage to work. But when I opened my eyes, it was Iris who was shaking my shoulder and smiling down at me.

'What is it?' I said in a panic, trying to gather my thoughts. 'Am I too late? Or are they all still here?'

It was nearly the end of my second week at the Hall, and the Vyes were entertaining guests at dinner. The gentlemen were in the billiard room, smoking and drinking brandy, while the ladies chatted over cards and tea in the drawing room. Jemima had told me to wait out of sight across the corridor, so that I could tidy up the rooms after the company had gone. It was well after midnight and, although I had sat down on a hard chair in a corner of the dining room, I had not been able to keep my eyes open a second longer.

'Keep your voice down,' Iris whispered. 'Don't worry, William told me you were here – no one else has seen you. I've just made hot chocolate for a couple of the ladies and he's taken it through. They probably won't be much longer.' (Being the still room maid, Iris prepared hot drinks for the house, as well as making bread and rolls, preserves, cakes and other delicious things, and waiting on the upper servants in Mrs Henderson's room.)

'I hope not.' I yawned and eased my aching back. Every bone in my body felt stiff and sore: my knees were blistered from those terrible hard floors, my arms red raw up to the elbow with scrubbing, and the skin on my hands all cracked and chapped from a constant dunking in icy water. I had been up since six o'clock that morning and felt decidedly sorry for myself.

'You'll get used to the work in the end,' Iris told me

sympathetically. 'I'll sit here for a while with you, if you like. Has Jemima gone off to bed?'

I nodded. 'You'll get used to her too,' Iris said. 'She can be a little – well, sharp, sometimes, but don't take it to heart.'

'I think she hates me,' I confessed. 'I seem to have offended her, and haven't the first idea what to do about it.'

Iris laughed. 'Oh, it's not your fault. She's only cross because she has to clean the servants' quarters, and that's something she considers beneath her dignity. It's only because we're one housemaid short that Mary picked Jemima to work with you. She thinks she's a cut above the rest of us, and she's very quick to take offence. But there's bound to be a new maid coming soon and then everything will be back to normal. So cheer up! Remember, it's Sunday tomorrow. We'll have the afternoon off.'

Then we heard the gentlemen coming back to join the ladies after their cigars, so I hurried off to tidy the billiard room, now it was empty. It was another half hour before the guests finally left, and another half hour on top of that before I was done with my work and could at last climb the endless staircase to our room. All I wanted was to sleep like the dead until morning (not so very far away now), but a storm was building up and the wind battered against the window beside me as though it was determined to break in – even though I had managed to stop the worst of the rattling with a handkerchief wedged into the frame. The noise made me feel restless and afraid as I drifted in and out of sleep, tossing and turning in my narrow bed. And then suddenly I was startled completely awake by the certain knowledge that somebody was there in the darkness with me, their face very close to my own and their breath cool upon my cheek.

I lay there for a few seconds, rigid with terror, staring wide-eyed into the pitch black while my heart hammered as though it would jump out of my chest. The room seemed to be full of strange noises: rustling, creaking, and a low moaning which was surely something other than the wind outside. At last, after what seemed like an eternity, I summoned up the courage to reach for the matchbox on the chair next to my bed. But by the time my trembling fingers had succeeded in lighting the candle, whoever – or whatever – had been leaning over me, was gone. All I could see were the humped, still shapes of Jemima, Becky and Iris, sleeping soundly through the night.

I kept the candle burning until it sputtered out in a pool of wax, only to doze off myself shortly before Mary knocked on the door at a quarter to six to wake us up. After we had done the early morning's work, we would be going to church in Stonemartin, the village which lay a mile or so beyond Swallowcliffe's gates, and then after dinner, most of us would have the whole afternoon off. I had not yet decided what to do with my free time; Mary had said I was free to explore the estate grounds as long as I kept out of sight if any of the family also happened to be walking there. (Lord Vye, in particular, did not like to come across any of us in the gardens.) Now, of course, I was too tired and nervous to know what to do with myself. I could not stop thinking about what had happened the previous night. Could I have imagined the whole thing? It seemed hard to believe in the bright daylight, with everyone going about their usual daily business around me. And then I remembered how utterly terrified I had felt on waking. No, someone – or something – had paid me a visit, I was sure of it.

After we maids had made all the beds, emptied the slops and chamber pots (my least favourite job) and taken away the early-morning trays, we went back to our room to prepare for going to church. The servants would be walking there while the Vyes arrived later on in their carriage. But now here was another problem for me: Jemima and Becky were tying on bonnets, laughing together as they jostled for position in front of the mirror. We had to wear our black dresses, but we could wear our own hats. (This surprised me, as I knew it was forbidden in many houses where the mistress did not want her servants looking too fine.) I had suffered the previous week, having to go to church bare-headed. The only thing

I had to wear was my work cap; all I needed was a duster and people would think I had come to give the place a spring clean! You will probably find it hard to believe that I did not even have a hat of my own, but the black straw Mother had given me had fallen to pieces the year before, and we had nothing with which to replace it. Luckily, Iris noticed me watching the other two and came to my rescue.

'Polly, this hat has never really suited me,' she said, bringing over a lovely black velvet bonnet, trimmed with forget-me-nots. 'Let me see how it looks on you.' She tugged the hat this way and that until she was quite satisfied, and then fixed it in place with a pin. 'Yes, I do believe it has found its rightful owner at last. Thank goodness! Now I can wear my straw with a clear conscience.'

I did not believe her for one second. Iris would have looked a picture whatever she wore, and those forget-me-nots would have brought out the blue of her eyes. I could not understand how I had first thought Jemima pretty; now I knew her a little better, the discontented look on her face and the downward turn of her mouth fairly spoilt her looks for me. But Iris was quite beautiful, all soft curves and peachy skin, and sweet-natured through and through. I could not think how to accept her gift and stood there awkwardly with tears in my eyes yet again, I have to confess. You are probably thinking me a pathetic creature, always weeping at the slightest thing, but sometimes unexpected kindness can make a person feel very sorry for herself.

By the time we were on our way to church, I had recovered myself enough to thank Iris properly. She put her arm through mine and we walked along together very companionably. 'Are you feeling quite well?' she asked me. 'You look white as a sheet this morning.'

I had not meant to tell anyone about my experience the night before, but before I knew where I was, the whole story began pouring out. I was hardly expecting Iris to believe me, but she listened closely to every word.

'You know what this means, don't you?' Jemima broke in, when I came to the end of my account. I had not realised that she and Becky had been walking close enough to overhear our conversation. 'Olive has met Ignatius! Well, I have often wondered whether any of us would.'

'Who is Ignatius?' I asked, quite encouraged that Jemima was taking an interest in me (and deciding to ignore the 'Olive'). 'What might he be doing in our bedroom, anyway?'

This was the story Jemima told, and it sent the shivers running up and down my spine. The third Lord Vye, His Lordship's grandfather, had established business interests in the West Indies. He had made a great deal of money from sugar plantations out there, and spent most of it rebuilding Swallowcliffe Hall in great style. Well, he returned from one of his regular trips overseas with a young Negro slave boy, aged about five or six, as a present for his wife. Apparently this child was a dear little thing and became a great success with the family; Lady Vye dressed him up in the finest clothes, petted him, and took him everywhere with her. It was soon quite the thing to have a black servant, which many people claimed was largely because of Lady Vye and her young page.

All went well until Ignatius began to grow into a young man, whereupon Lady Vye began to find him less charming and eventually tired of him completely, dismissing him from her service. He worked in the kitchen for a while, but then it was decided he should be sent back to the West Indies, to take up his former life as a slave on the plantations. Of course this must have been a terrible shock for the poor lad, because now he thought of England as his home and could not remember much about his early childhood (which by all accounts was a harsh and miserable one, for the plantation manager did not treat his slaves well). The very morning Ignatius was to be taken to Dover and put upon a ship bound for the West Indies, he was found dead in his room – hanging by a silk scarf, the last remnant of his fine wardrobe.

'And they say his ghost will haunt Swallowcliffe for ever, swearing vengeance on all who live there for the terrible wrong he suffered,' Jemima finished dramatically.

I thought back to that low moaning and rustling of the previous night, and shuddered. It was hard for me to concentrate on the sermon in church after hearing such a dismal, sad story, though I certainly prayed hard enough for that poor boy's spirit to rest in peace. Why had he chosen to visit me? And would he come again? Neither of these were particularly comforting thoughts. That afternoon, Iris and I went for a walk around the gardens and she showed me some of her favourite things: a winding gravel path through the rose garden; a mossy stone fountain beside the summerhouse; the little marble statue of Eustacia Vye, who had died of rheumatic fever at the age of two, nearly a hundred years before. Then we sat for a while in the boathouse on the far side of the lake, a rather forlorn and musty place in the middle of winter.

'Don't listen to Jemima's stories,' Iris said, squeezing my arm. 'This is a happy place. Everything's bound to seem a little strange at first, but you'll soon be feeling quite at home – just wait and see.'

She had done her best to cheer me up, but I was still dreading going to bed that night. When at last I couldn't put off retiring any longer, I lay there rigid with fear, listening to every tiny noise in the whole of that creaking old house. I could not stop thinking about all the other servants who had lived and worked at Swallowcliffe, besides poor Ignatius. How many girls had slept in this room over the years, and what stories did they have to tell? There must have been many who had felt just as lonely and miserable as I did now – worse, maybe, since they might have been beaten or half-starved in crueller times. My thoughts ran away with themselves until the air around me seemed to ring with desperate voices clamouring for attention, determined not to let me rest, and I had to put the pillow over my head to try and drown them out.

The next morning, I was a sorry bundle of nerves, half dead with tiredness. As I swept out the grate in Miss Harriet's bedroom, all of a sudden there came a long, low sigh from somewhere near the window. I dropped the dustpan and brush and screamed out loud.

'Who's there?' said a surprised voice, and the curtain was drawn back to reveal Harriet herself, wrapped up in a blanket, and settled comfortably on the window seat with her little dog, Nelson. I had seen her at prayers in the chapel and noticed her particularly at church the day before: she was Lord Vye's younger daughter and near my age, I thought. Not what you would call a pretty girl, but striking, with thick auburn hair and something very lively and likeable about her expression.

'I'm so sorry, Miss,' I said, hastily picking up my things. 'You startled me. I'm just laying your fire and then I'll be off.'

'You startled me back,' she said, though she didn't sound

too cross about it. 'Wait! Come here for a moment and see this.'

I went over to the window, though to be honest I would sooner have got on with my work because I was behind already. The hot water jugs and tea trays were still to be taken around before breakfast, not to mention all the servants' rooms which Jemima and I would have to tackle afterwards. I forgot about them as soon as I glanced outside, however. Miss Harriet's bedroom faced the park, and a fine stag was standing a little way apart from the rest of the herd. He looked like some creature out of a fairy tale, half hidden in the early-morning mist among the pale trunks of the silver birch trees. As we watched, he pawed the ground with his hooves and bellowed.

'I think he is trying to attract a female,' Harriet told me. 'They don't seem very interested, do they? I can't see why not. He looks a handsome fellow to me.'

'Perhaps he has no conversation,' I said, forgetting myself for a moment.

Well, that made her laugh. 'Can you sit with me for a while?' she said, patting the seat beside her. 'I feel like some company this morning.'

'I would love to, Miss,' I said (which was quite true), 'but there's so much work to be done! I should have got your fire going by now, for one thing – you must be half frozen to death.' I fetched a quilt from the bed to make her more comfortable. Oh, she did look snug! I'd have given my eye teeth to be so warm and cosy, sitting there beside her, and nothing to do with the rest of the day but watch deer and stroll around the estate.

'You are new here, aren't you?' she asked as I tucked her in. 'What is your name? How old are you?'

'Polly, Miss,' I said, having decided to give up on Olive once and for all. 'I am fourteen.'

'I shall be fourteen in July!' she said, as if it were the strangest thing in the world that we should be so close in age. (I did not have the heart to tell her that she could never catch me up: come the summer, I would be fifteen.) 'And my name is Harriet, as you probably know. I hope we shall be friends.'

I nearly laughed out loud at this. The idea of me being friends with Lord Vye's daughter! I might not have been at the Hall long, but I had quickly realised that to most of the family, we servants were invisible, apart from the evidence of the work we did. I had tried my best to melt into the wall when Lord Vye passed me in the corridor the other day, but he looked straight through me anyway. Still, that's Miss Harriet for you: she has her own way of looking at the world.

As we talked, I noticed that Harriet had torn her night-gown, climbing up on the window seat. She told me that

Agnes, the young ladies' maid who attended to her and her older sister Miss Eugenie, had complained to Lady Vye about the amount of mending she was expected to do, and that Lady Vye had had sharp words with Harriet about it. She was not nearly so careful with her clothes as Eugenie. So I offered to darn the nightgown if she wanted, without Agnes or anyone else having to know about it. I had had enough of hemming dusters and sheets, to be truthful, and was glad of the chance to show what I could do. When I had finished, no one would know the nightgown had ever been torn in the first place.

'Now I am sure we shall be friends,' Harriet said, quickly changing out of her nightgown and into another. 'I wish *you* could be my maid, Polly! Agnes is always so cross and disapproving.'

I shall be glad enough to stay as under housemaid for the time being, I thought, once Miss Harriet's fire was alight and I was hurrying along to the next bedroom with her nightgown hidden under my apron bib. I spent the rest of that morning trying to catch up with myself, for there was plenty to be done and now I was later than ever. I did not have a chance to sit down to my sewing until late that night, when everyone else had gone to bed and I was the only one left in the housemaids' room.

To be honest, I was glad of an excuse to put off going to bed. I was beginning to think that our attic room was

40

haunted by all kinds of unhappy spirits, and that they had chosen me to listen to their sorrows. It was a heavy burden to bear.

FOUR

Keep yourself quiet under whatever storms may be brought to bear upon you; bide your time, *then when the anger or displeasure has passed, ask for the opportunity to make your explanations. But never forgetting the respectful service demanded of you as the Lord's servant.*

From *Thoughts for Servants*, Mrs W. H. Wigley, 1882

It was hard to get out of bed on those cold, dark, winter mornings, especially when I had passed a restless night; I usually managed to doze off what seemed like only minutes before Mary woke us up. 'Up you get, sleepy-head!' Iris called a couple of days later, pinching my toes under the bedclothes.

I forced my head up off the pillow and then fumbled underneath it for my locket, as usual. We were not allowed any jewellery, so I kept the chain hidden under my clothes in the daytime, held it tight while I said my prayers at night, and always slept with it tucked out of sight beneath the pillow.

'Whatever is the matter?' Iris asked as I tore the blanket and sheet off my bed and flapped them about in the air.

'My locket has gone!' I said, wide awake now. I got down on all fours and began feeling over the loose floor-boards, in case it had dropped down somewhere. 'Where can it be?'

'Mrs Henderson has probably confiscated it,' Jemima said, already slipping her feet into her shoes. 'You know we are not allowed to wear jewellery. You had better hope she will eventually let you have it back.' And she gave me an odd little smile as she swept out of the door.

I stared after her, trying to make sense of what she had said. I had always been very careful to let no one see my necklace, but Jemima did not seem at all surprised to hear about it. And why on earth should Mrs Henderson take it away in the middle of the night? Then all at once, everything became clear. There had been no ghostly black boy bending over my bed a few nights ago! It was a real, live person, somebody who meant me harm, and last night she had been on the prowl again. Now I knew exactly what had happened to my locket – Ignatius had had nothing to do with it. Suddenly I was filled with such a rush of anger that I fairly shook from head to foot. How dare Jemima even touch it! If she had still been in the room, I don't know what I would have done.

'Come on now or you really will be late,' Iris said, helping me up. 'Whatever you've lost, it can't have vanished into thin air. We can look for it later.'

'You don't understand,' I whispered urgently. 'Jemima's stolen it, I know she has!'

Iris stared at me in astonishment for a moment, and then she said quietly, 'Come to the still room before breakfast.' We could hardly discuss the matter in front of Becky.

I dressed in a daze, tying on the rough apron I wore to protect my clothes from the coal dust and powdery ashes while I laid the fires. Usually I enjoyed coaxing the flames into life and warming my poor numb fingers when there was a good blaze going – although I never felt comfortable tiptoeing past a person asleep in bed. (I should have hated to have someone creeping around me in the darkness!) This morning, however, I could think of nothing but my locket, and what possible reason Jemima could have had for taking it. Why did she hate me so much?

'How do you know the locket's been stolen?' Iris asked me, when I came to the still room a couple of hours later. I had the excuse of fetching a fresh pot of tea for the servants' hall, so we had a few seconds to talk. 'Are you sure you have not dropped it somewhere? And who's to say Jemima took it, anyway?'

I shook my head. 'You should have seen the look on her face this morning. She has something to do with it, sure as eggs is eggs!'

Iris still looked doubtful. 'She's never done anything like that before, so far as I know. And you can't go accusing her without any proof.'

'Won't you help me get it back?' I asked her. 'Please, Iris! That locket means everything to me. All I want to do is take a quick look through Jemima's things – she won't even know I was there. If I can't find it, then I'll never mention the matter again.'

'I don't hold with searching through someone's private belongings,' Iris said. 'I'll keep a lookout for you, but that's as far as I'll go and I'm still not very happy about it. You can have ten minutes in our room – I'll wait on the staircase to stop anyone coming up. And you'd better not be wrong, is all I can say.'

'Oh, thank you, thank you!' I hugged her. 'I know exactly the right time. We can slip upstairs after midday dinner, when we're meant to be fetching the mending. I shall find my locket, you'll see!'

I stood in front of Jemima's chest of drawers, quaking in my shoes. Iris was right: I shouldn't be rifling through things that didn't belong to me. But then I remembered what I hoped to find and hardened my heart. Jemima shared the chest with Becky, having the bottom two drawers to herself. Steeling myself, I tugged open the first and began carefully looking through the piles of neatly-folded clothes inside. I felt in the fingers of gloves and toes of stockings (happening to notice that Jemima had a good deal more of both of these than I did) for a locket-shaped bulge. Nothing! There was no sign of anything like a jewellery box, no little purse under that pile of lace handkerchiefs – in fact, nothing particularly personal at all, apart from two hatpins, a lace garter, a couple of letters and the black paper silhouette of a young lady that might have been Jemima herself, slipped between the pages of a bible. I felt a little ashamed of myself for even noticing them, but I *had* to find my locket. Where on earth had she hidden it? It must be there somewhere!

The bottom drawer was even harder to open than the top one. At last I managed to pull it free and searched feverishly under the stack of chemises, drawers, night-gowns and petticoats. Still no success, yet I could not give up. I ran my fingers under the mattress on Jemima's bed, shook her pillow and untucked the blanket. Time was running out and I became more desperate as the minutes ticked away. Had Iris been right after all? Was this all for nothing? I turned back to the chest and began searching the first drawer again. This was where the locket had to be: there were more bits and bobs here than anywhere else.

'And exactly what do you think you are doing, may I ask?' An icy voice cut through the air, crystal-clear. I whirled around – and there, to my horror, stood Jemima in the doorway, glaring at me, fit to kill. What could I say? The drawer was open in front of me and its contents spilled out all higgledy-piggledy. In a few seconds, she had crossed the room and yanked me to my feet. 'Why are you interfering with my belongings?'

'I am looking for my locket,' I said, meeting her furious gaze full on. 'It's mine and I want it back. I know you've taken it.'

'Oh, do you indeed?' she hissed. 'Well, the only thief I can see in this room is standing in front of me. You can come with me and explain yourself to Mrs Henderson. Let's see what she has to say about the matter!' She grabbed hold of my elbow so tightly her fingers nearly met in the middle, and marched me off towards the door.

Iris was nowhere to be seen on the staircase. Whatever had happened to her? Why hadn't she warned me Jemima was coming? I didn't know what to think, or how on earth I was going to account for myself. Taking a sideways glance at Jemima's face, I sensed that underneath the anger, she was delighted to be landing me in such trouble; she was fairly quivering with joy at the thought of the dressing-down I would get from Mrs Henderson. However, although I had not found the locket yet, I was still certain that she had taken it, and somehow that gave me courage.

The housekeeper was sorting through piles of sheets in the huge linen closets on the landing. She told Jemima and me to go to her room and wait for her there; I had the feeling she was not best pleased to be disturbed.

'And what did you think you were doing, looking through somebody else's chest of drawers?' she asked me, when Jemima had told her the whole story.

'Please, ma'am, I had mislaid a chemise that needed mending and thought it might have got muddled up with Jemima's things,' I said humbly. Jemima made as if to speak, but then stopped abruptly. I knew she could not risk mentioning the locket. If she had told Mrs Henderson I had accused her of stealing it, then the housekeeper might order a full-scale search for the thing and perhaps it would be found after all. So she had not been quite as clever as she thought.

Nevertheless, I was on my knees by the time Mrs Henderson had finished with me. I should have asked Jemima's permission before searching through her clothes; I had a great deal to learn about respect for my elders and betters; if anything was reported missing in our bedroom, I would be dismissed immediately – and so on, and so on. The long and short of it was that I had two more weeks to prove myself before my month's notice was up. If she did not see a distinct improvement in my conduct, I would not be offered a permanent position.

'Now get on with your work,' she said. 'Jemima, you can stay behind for a minute.'

I let myself out of the room, my legs shaking – and you will probably think I am quite mad to do what I did next, given Mrs Henderson's warning, but while I was standing there in front of her, I had suddenly remembered something rather strange from my argy-bargy upstairs with Jemima. When I had told her that I was looking for my locket, her eyes had immediately flickered over to the chair beside her bed. Why should she have glanced there in particular, unless it was her secret hiding place? So instead of going straight to the housemaids' sitting room to get on with my sewing, I dashed up the back staircase to our bedroom. Jemima would be safely out of the way for a few minutes in Mrs Henderson's room, and such a chance might not come my way again. Quickly I turned the chair upside down, expecting to see my locket somehow tied underneath. There was no sign of it. I ran my fingers over the joints and even resorted to shaking the chair, in case perhaps my necklace had been slipped inside a hollow leg. At last I had to admit defeat and set it back in place, quite discouraged that my wonderful idea should have come to nothing.

And that was when I felt a badly-fitting floorboard creak and move beneath my foot. Dropping to my knees, I pushed and prodded along the length of it, and saw one end of the board move as I pressed down on the other. Was there time for me to lever it right up? Jemima might be coming back to tidy her things at any moment. Frantically, I pulled out one of my hairpins and started to work away at the floorboard, one ear cocked to listen out for her step on the staircase.

Yes! At last I had a finger under a corner of the board, and then in a matter of seconds, the whole thing came up in my hands. And there was my precious locket, shining cheerfully up at me from between the dusty joists in its hidey-hole beneath. I snatched it up, fastened the chain around my neck and tucked the locket under my clothes – feeling whole again now that its familiar shape was pressing against my skin. Then I hurried back downstairs, deciding I had got off lightly, all in all.

'Polly! Are you all right? What happened?' Iris was climbing up the staircase as I came down. 'Jemima said Mary wanted to see me urgently. I had to go down, there was nothing else to be done, but I tried to make as much noise as possible to warn you. Did you hear me?'

'No,' I said, 'but it doesn't matter. Look!' And I pulled out the locket. 'I must mind my Ps and Qs now, though, Iris. I can't afford to put a foot wrong if I'm to be kept on here.'

'Then get back to work this minute!' she said, smiling

and flapping a dishcloth at me. 'Go on, and quick about it!'

I laughed and hugged her, feeling suddenly light-hearted in spite of everything. I had got my locket back, and while I might have made an enemy at Swallowcliffe, at least I was sure of a friend too. Iris had helped me, I had got the better of Jemima, and our bedroom was not haunted after all. Things were looking up.

I really did try my very best over the next week or so. Jemima did not bother me so much now; I despised her, after what she had done to me. Let her scowl all she wanted, I would just ignore it and get on with my work. She must have known I had retrieved the locket, but we never spoke of it again. Only, one morning when we were making the beds together, she pulled my arm as I went past and whispered in my ear, 'You'll get your comeuppance soon enough, madam. Don't think I shall forget what you've done in a hurry.' The strength of feeling in her voice frightened me, but then I reminded myself that she had done me wrong, not the other way around, and dismissed her remark for the petty spite it was.

I was getting to know William a little better too. We were meant to keep away from the menservants, but I would often bump into him early of a morning when I was laying the fires downstairs and he was filling up the coal buckets. There was never anyone else about at the time, so we could have a chat quite safely (we were not supposed to talk to each other in the front of the house, as a rule). He looked much more ordinary then, not being in livery or having to powder his hair until it was time to serve the family breakfast. He said the powder made his head itch something terrible, and I thought he looked much more handsome without it; such thick, wavy brown hair he had, and brown eyes like mine that were usually crinkled up in a smile. He would often make me laugh with some tale about what had happened at dinner the night before, and it got my day off to a very good start if I should happen to see him.

I was also becoming quite friendly with Miss Harriet, as she had predicted. She took to following me around in the middle of the day when things were not so busy, asking me all sorts of questions about my work. Perhaps she was bored. Her old nurse, Nanny Roberts, spent most of the time looking after Master John, and she didn't seem to have many friends her own age; John was too young to be much of a companion for her, and Eugenie too busy turning herself into an eligible young lady. I had to show her the marble sluice in a cupboard along the corridor where we emptied away the slops, which she'd never even noticed before, and explain the use of everything inside my cleaning box: blackleading for the fireplaces, soft soap and silver sand to scrub the floorboards (you couldn't risk getting them too wet) – even a slice of stale bread for taking marks off the wallpaper. She particularly liked my dustpan, which had a hole for my thumb and a holder for my candle so that I could use it with one hand in the dark. I am sure she would have been a lot less taken with the thing had she had to use it every day, but decided not to say so.

There would soon be no time for any more of our cosy chats, however, because it was shortly Miss Eugenie's eighteenth birthday and we would be rushed off our feet from morning till night. A large party of guests was staying at the Hall, including Lord Vye's two sisters and their families, and Master Edward and Master Rory were coming home too. There would be dinner parties and dancing to entertain the fine company, and hunting and shooting no doubt, for those who liked that sort of thing – and then there was to be a grand masked ball to mark the birthday itself.

'You are bound to like my brothers,' Harriet informed me. 'All our maids fall in love with one or the other. Some people say Edward is more handsome, but Rory can charm the birds out of the trees – and he is a cavalry officer, which is too dashing for words. If you saw him in his uniform, you would just die on the spot.'

'Then we had better hope he'll not be wearing it this

weekend,' I said, and we laughed. I was brushing out Miss Harriet's hair; she said I had a lighter hand than Agnes. 'And is Master Edward in the army too?'

'No, he is studying at Oxford University. He finishes his degree in the summer and then he will come back and learn how to run the estate, since he is going to inherit it all when my father dies. So he will soon be looking for a wife.' She sighed. 'And there's Eugenie already after a husband.'

'But she is so young! There will be plenty of time for that, surely?'

'She wants to be mistress of her own house. Anyway, all the best girls get snapped up in their first season, or so my stepmother says.'

I had only seen Eugenie from a distance but, to be honest, I did not find her quite as beautiful as everyone else seemed to think. She reminded me of a painted porcelain doll, with that rosebud mouth and her round blue eyes set so wide apart. Oh, I am sure she had lovely manners and she could certainly sing and play the piano beautifully, but in my opinion her face seemed to lack some spark of expression to make it interesting. Give me Miss Harriet any day of the week, for all her red hair and freckles. Strange, though; you would never have taken them for sisters.

Harriet was looking rather mournfully at her reflection

in the mirror. 'Just think,' I said, to cheer her up, 'you will be in Miss Eugenie's place in a few years' time, going through to dinner on the arm of some dashing young man! I am sure you will look very elegant.' And I piled up her hair to see how it suited her. In fact, this made her chin seem a little too – obvious, somehow, but a few pretty ringlets would probably soften the effect.

'I would sooner be dead!' Harriet said crossly, shaking her hair out of my hands. 'Having to make polite conversation with some boring creature my stepmother thinks is suitable! Eugenie told me she dozed off when she was sitting next to the Honourable Henry Cavendish last week, but when she woke up he was still droning on about his collection of interesting fungi and she hadn't missed a thing.'

We both laughed some more at this, and I decided that perhaps I had misjudged Eugenie. 'Do you ever want to get married, Polly?' Harriet asked, which made me think a bit.

'I am not sure that I do,' I said at last. My parents had been happy enough together, but it was a hard life for my mother, having four children to bring up on very little money – even before my father died. And what if the man I married took to drink, or turned out to have a bad temper? Besides, if I took a husband I would have to leave service, and I was certainly not ready for that just yet. It seemed to me that if I could work my way up the ladder and become one of the Upper Ten one day (as the upper servants were known), that would be a very pleasant sort of life. My own room with a fireplace, nicely furnished, my own linen napkin in a silver ring, and a good wage with plenty of tips! It would have to be a fine man who could compete with that.

'I am never getting married,' Harriet said decisively. 'I shall keep house for my brother Rory, and own a pack of beagles and hunt all day long. Will you come and be my housekeeper, Polly?'

'Certainly,' I said – so that was decided.

The very next day, however, something took place which was to change my prospects at the Hall completely. Nothing to do with Jemima, either: I brought about this disaster all by myself. Perhaps it was because I was feeling happier, and that made me feel more confident than I should have done. I can think of no other reason why I should have been so stupid.

This is how it happened. Mary checked her cleaning box before tea the next afternoon and realised that she must have left a duster in Lady Vye's sitting room upstairs. Luckily, the family was occupied with their own tea in the main drawing room, but Mary was in a quandary because Mrs Henderson wanted to see her right away and she had no time to retrieve the duster. I offered to fetch it for her, trying to be helpful, so Mary told me to hurry straight there and back, and no messing about along the way. Off I went, and sure enough, there was the duster on Lady Vye's writing table. I picked it up, and then couldn't resist a closer look at the table, with its pretty design of flowers all inlaid in different woods.

Oh, why hadn't I listened to Mary? It would have saved me a great deal of trouble. But it is easy to be wise after the event, and my eye had been caught by an exquisite porcelain figurine standing in one corner. The day before, I had heard Mary grumbling to Becky about Lady Vye and these figurines of hers. She had four of them, a present from His Lordship; they each represented a season, and she liked to keep a different one on her table each week to look at while she wrote her letters. Mary was always forgetting to change them around; she had plenty of other things on her mind. Which season was this? I wondered, picking up the china figure. (What *was* I thinking of?) It was a young country girl in a sprigged muslin frock, carrying a thick sheaf of corn. Autumn, most probably, rather than summer. Of course, I should never have touched the thing! I was not even allowed to dust the top of the writing table; polishing its legs was the furthest I could go. Handling anything so precious as this ornament was strictly forbidden.

Suddenly, the door burst open with a crash, and in

rushed Miss Harriet. I was so startled by the noise, and already so guilty besides, that the figurine flew out of my hand. It fell on the floor and cracked into three or four pieces, the dainty head with its fair curls rolling away from me across the carpet.

I stared at Harriet, frozen with horror. She looked down at the broken china and then back at me. There was nothing to be said. We could hear Lady Vye's voice calling from somewhere close by as she followed her stepdaughter up the stairs. I was in the most terrible trouble, and we both knew it.

FIVE

Still not saying a word, Harriet put a finger to her lips as some sort of signal to me and then darted forward to gather up the pieces of porcelain. By the time Lady Vye had entered the room, she had turned and was hurrying back to meet her, holding out the evidence of my crime. I followed, frightened half to death to think what might happen next.

'I am so sorry, *belle-mère*,' Harriet said (and she looked it, too). 'As I went past the desk, my sleeve caught one of your little figures and it fell on the floor. Please forgive me! I know how much you love them.'

I could not believe it! She was taking the blame for my wrongdoing. It was such a kind, brave thing to do that, for a moment, I was speechless. But I could not stand by and let someone else pay for my mistake. 'M'lady, I ought to tell you that—' I began in a quavering voice, clutching the duster to my chest.

'When was your opinion called for?' Lady Vye broke in, staring at me in astonishment. 'I am not in the habit of being lectured by a housemaid. Kindly go about your duties elsewhere.'

What else could I do? Harriet would not even look in my direction. After one last glance at her determined face, I curtseyed and went out of the room. I could hear Lady Vye telling her stepdaughter what a clumsy, unladylike creature she was before I had even reached the door, and my heart bled for her. I did not have the courage to turn back, though, and hurried along to give Mary back the wretched duster and think what to do next.

Four o'clock tea had quickly become my favourite time of the day. The maids' sitting room was such a pleasant place, with a view out over the kitchen garden and sturdy, comfortable furniture. The old armchairs with their faded flowery covers had originally come from the family drawing room: I much preferred them to the spindly gilt and brocade chairs that stood there now. Iris would lay a starched white cloth over the work table and we would have plum cake with our tea, and bread and butter with jam from the still room. It was half an hour of peace before the evening rush, and Jemima was never so sharp with me when other people were around.

This afternoon, however, I could take no pleasure in anything. What on earth would be happening to poor Harriet? She must have realised that I would lose my job immediately for breaking the ornament (I had previously told her about my warning from Mrs Henderson), and had risked her stepmother's anger to protect me. I felt more ashamed of myself for letting her take the blame than I did for being so naughty in the first place – too ashamed to confess to anyone what had happened. All I could do was stare into my teacup and wonder how I could ever have been so stupid and thoughtless.

At supper time, William brought the news that Harriet had been made to stand in a corner of the library for three hours, and had just this minute been sent to bed without anything to eat. It must have been humiliating; Harriet was too old to be treated like a child in this way. I could not bear to think of her standing there, quite alone with an aching back and tired legs, and nothing to look at but row upon row of musty books – probably hungry and thirsty into the bargain. And all because of me! I blushed so fiercely with shame that it was a wonder nobody noticed.

'What is she meant to have done this time?' said Mr Wilkins, the under butler. 'Poor lass! Do you know, Her Ladyship ordered me to fetch two saucers last Sunday luncheon for Miss Harriet's elbows. She had to sit there like that for the whole meal, to teach her to keep them off the table.'

'She is trying to break the girl's spirit, that's what it's all about,' Mary said. 'They are two strong characters, and neither will give way to the other. Mind you, Lady Vye has made a good job of Miss Eugenie: lovely manners, that young lady has, and all the accomplishments. No one could accuse Her Ladyship of neglecting her duties as a stepmother. And if she cannot love the girls quite so much as she does Master John, that is only to be expected. He is her own flesh and blood, after all.'

And then Iris appeared from the housekeeper's room with the full story, which she had overheard from the upper servants. Lady Vye had given Mrs Henderson the broken figurine to see if it could be mended, and told her about Miss Harriet's disgrace. To my surprise, the house-keeper and the cook seemed to have taken Harriet's side even more strongly than Mr Wilkins. But Mary told us that Miss Harriet had been a favourite in the kitchen since she was small; she had her own little apron and bowl and would spend hours there, making pastry and biscuits. Apparently, Mrs Bragg had just now told one of the kitchenmaids to put together a plate of game pie and pickled onions so that William could smuggle it up to Miss Harriet's bedroom. Fancy the fearsome knife thrower, thinking of that!

Harriet was sitting up in bed, reading by the light of a candle lamp, when I went into her room with hot water and towels later that evening. 'Oh, Miss,' I said, hurrying over to her. 'However can I thank you? But why did you do it? You should have let me confess and take the punishment, not you.'

'Then you would have been dismissed,' she said, all matter-of-fact. 'And that cannot happen to stepdaughters, or I would have been sent away a long time ago. Don't worry, it's all over and done with now.'

Sadly for both of us, however, this was not the case. The very next morning at breakfast, Mary told us she had just heard from Mrs Henderson that Lady Vye had given Harriet's old nanny notice to leave. A new governess would be coming in her place, to teach Miss Harriet how to behave. Even Mary was shocked by this, despite her support for Lady Vye. 'Poor Miss Harriet!' she said, chewing her lip more anxiously than ever. 'Nanny Roberts must be the nearest thing to a mother she's ever had. And what about Master John? He'll be heartbroken.'

'So there are to be no more babies in the house,' Becky said, looking meaningfully at Jemima. 'Well, I can't say I'm surprised, what with the Vyes in separate bedrooms and never going near each other so far as anyone can see.'

'That is quite enough!' Mary was outraged. 'There is no call for gossip of such kind here, thank you very much. If you want to spread tittle-tattle, you had better go and work in the laundry.'

What a deal of trouble had come about because of one little china figurine! Mary said that she had heard Lady Vye had decided to dismiss Nanny Roberts some time ago (this information came from Miss de Courcy, Lady Vye's maid), but I knew her leaving was meant as an extra punishment for Harriet and would never forgive myself for helping bring it about. However, I was soon taken up with troubles enough of my own. Mary told me to report to Mrs Henderson's room after breakfast. There was a terrible sinking feeling in the pit of my stomach; as soon as I saw her face, I knew I was right to fear the worst.

'I thought I made myself perfectly clear the last time I had cause to speak to you,' she said. 'You had two weeks to improve. Did you not want to carry on working here?'

'Oh yes, ma'am! I do, very much. I tried to—'

'Enough!' she snapped. 'That does not matter now. I

have had to hear from Lady Vye herself that you have acted impertinently towards her! You should have left the room the minute Her Ladyship appeared, instead of addressing her directly. I must have told you a hundred times never to speak unless you are spoken to. Do you think I enjoyed having to stand there and listen to an account of your shameful behaviour? Well, do you?'

'No, ma'am,' I whispered.

'You have disappointed me a great deal, Polly Perkins. If we were not expecting company, I would have sent you off to pack your bags immediately. But we are short-staffed as it is and there are guests arriving today. Stay until the ball is over and you can have a full month's wages and your train fare home. I can't say fairer than that – it's only another few days. Now get out of my sight.'

'Yes, ma'am,' I said, and let myself out. I walked back down the corridor towards the servants' hall in a daze, and then the full force of what had just happened came home to me and I had to lean against the wall for a moment to catch my breath. I had been dismissed! I was to be sent away in disgrace, with only a month's wages to give my mother and no decent character reference to help me get another job. This was a disaster. We were in desperate need of money at home: Mother had had to cut the toes out of my sister Lizzie's boots to give more room for her feet and she was counting on my help to buy new ones. And the shame of it, coming back to our village like that with my tail between my legs, when I had left so proudly! Whatever would we tell the neighbours? And how could I say goodbye to Iris and William, and Miss Harriet?

The other housemaids were setting off upstairs to clean the bedrooms. I could tell from the way they looked at me – Becky curious but not unkind, Jemima triumphant – that Mary must have told them my situation.

'There you are, Polly,' Mary said to me. 'Do your best over the next few days and you may still get a decent character. We need you.' And she put an arm round my shoulder to shepherd me along.

It was kind of her to speak to me like that, but I knew she was worried that I would not see the point in trying any more, and there was a great deal of work to be done. All those guest bedrooms had to be cleaned and the beds made every day, and several of the ladies who were coming to stay were not bringing servants with them. Mary and Becky would be maiding the married ladies, Jemima the single, and many of their regular duties would fall on my shoulders. I have always worked hard, though; it is in my nature to do the best I can, no matter what the circumstances, and I was not going to change now.

The Hall did look lovely that day, ready for the house party and the ball to come. There were fires, clean towels and linen in every bedroom, fresh writing paper and candles on each desk, and huge bowls of flowers on all the gleaming side tables, despite the season. Lord Vye had supervised the building of three hothouses the year before, and the gardeners had been raising orchids, lilies and freesias all winter. We couldn't help pausing now and then to breathe in their fragrance, alongside the familiar Swallowcliffe smells of beeswax polish, woodsmoke and baking.

I had been so proud to come here, yet now all this beauty and comfort was like a knife in my heart. 'Look what you will be leaving behind,' the rooms seemed to whisper to me as I walked through them. 'Such luxury is not for the likes of you. Go back and skivvy in some humble place where you belong.'

The rest of the day passed in a dream. Our guests began arriving in the afternoon; suddenly the house was full of elegantly-dressed ladies and gentlemen, and all the welcoming hustle and bustle that came with them. Coachmen and footmen hurried to and fro with armfuls of luggage, while we showed the visitors to their rooms and made sure they had everything they needed. Mrs Henderson seemed to be in a hundred places at once: Lady So and So's hatbox had been mislaid on the journey from the station; Lord What'shisname would like another pillow and the windows opened in his room – the

Countess, however, was nowhere near warm enough and wanted the fire banking up. Then on top of everything else, the Dowager Duchess's maid had forgotten to pack her diamonds and a footman had to be sent back to London by the very next train to pick them up. Not such a great disaster, though you might have thought so for all the fuss and squawking that went on. I could not help feeling a little bitter with all the worries that were staring me in the face. The way things had turned out, I should have owned up to breaking the figurine in the first place and saved Miss Harriet the trouble.

I did not see Harriet to talk to all day as she was taken up with her cousins, and I could not tell Iris what had happened either, since she was too busy to set foot outside the still room. Then in the evening we were rushed off our feet, taking up cans of hot water for the guests' hip baths and making sure each room had plenty of soap and towels. Dinner always started at eight o'clock – Lord Vye hated to be late – and Mrs Henderson told us maids we could watch the company going in to the dining room from the upstairs landing, as long as we were careful to keep out of sight. I saw William down there, looking very smart in his best livery, and hoped his poor head wasn't itching too much. The second footman, Thomas, stood opposite him on the other side of the double doors, and the gentlemen and ladies went through between them, two by two. Lord Vye led the way with an elderly duchess hanging off his arm, followed by Her Ladyship, who was escorted by some officer or general with hardly enough dinner jacket for all his rows of medals. She was wearing the most gorgeous blue velvet gown, and diamonds sparkled around her neck and in her hair.

'Master Edward will be a catch for one lucky girl some day,' Becky said, peeking at him through the banisters. 'In line to inherit the whole estate, and handsome to boot! I don't know why he has to be so solemn and serious all the time.' It was true: there *was* a rather brooding air about Edward's face. His eyes were dark and deep-set, and he did not seem to smile very often.

'Isn't Miss Eugenie a picture?' Mary sighed, and we all agreed that Agnes had done her proud. She did look lovely, with her hair piled up in a mass of dark ringlets, dressed in pale yellow silk and pearls – like some fresh spring flower, I thought to myself. 'A lamb to the slaughter,' Jemima remarked, which was just the sort of thing she *would* say. Miss Eugenie looked more like a cat who'd got the cream to me. A fair-haired young man was taking her into dinner and paying her a great deal of attention, although I couldn't help noticing that he had a boil on the back of his neck and not much chin to speak of.

'Back to work!' Mary said at last, when all the guests had

gone through to the dining room. There must have been ten extra bedrooms to attend to, and they wouldn't tidy themselves. For much of the evening, gales of laughter had come floating down the corridor from the nursery, where Miss Harriet was entertaining her younger cousins. I was hurrying past the room a couple of hours later with some clean towels when suddenly the door burst open and a rabble of children came tumbling out, most of them riding on the back of a young man on all fours with tousled chestnut hair, who was roaring like a lion. He suddenly reared up with a particularly fearsome growl and Master John fell off, shrieking with delight, which only seemed to add to the general enjoyment. It was hard not to smile at the sight: John was such a sweet child, for all the world like the boy blowing bubbles on the Pear's soap picture, with his blond curls and dimpled chin. I could see the poor nurserymaid in the doorway behind, wringing her hands with anxiety, and Harriet, carrying a fat moon-faced baby who was laughing louder than anyone.

'Oh, Polly, this is Rory!' she cried as soon as she saw me. 'He has arrived at last!'

The young man struggled to his feet, shaking off the last few riders. 'I am delighted to make your acquaintance, Polly,' he said, somewhat out of breath, and then took my hand and pressed it to his lips. I wasn't quite sure what to do, not being in the habit of having my hand kissed by a gentleman; besides, he had made me drop the towels in a heap on the floor. So I muttered some hasty reply and curtseyed before stooping to pick them up – upon which we cracked heads together, as he had bent to do the very same thing! I was in some confusion by now, especially as it was a hard blow and I knew it must have hurt him too (although he had no one to blame but himself). The children, of course, thought all this was very funny.

Master Rory managed to recover his wits more quickly than I did. 'Look at all the trouble I've caused,' he said, bundling the towels untidily back in my arms. 'You are probably thinking I should be downstairs, quietly eating my dinner and making polite conversation, instead of whipping these poor little children into such a pitch of excitement they will never get to sleep tonight.'

Of course, he was perfectly right – the very thought was running through my head at that precise moment.

'You see, I can read your mind,' he said, looking at me so mischievously that I did not know where to put myself. 'You may have no secrets from me, pretty Polly. But I could not help being late, for various reasons, and Her Ladyship hates to have dinner interrupted. I was thinking of sloping down to the kitchen in a minute and asking Mrs Bragg to let me have something on a tray. Goddard is busy in the dining room, no doubt.'

71

'Oh, Rory, don't be ridiculous!' Harriet interrupted. 'How can you think of going anywhere near the kitchen in the middle of supper? You might think you can wind Mrs Bragg round your little finger, but she'll have you hanging from a meat hook in no time, I assure you.'

That was true enough. At dinnertime that day, I had heard the upper servants discussing the evening's menu: there were to be two different types of soup and turbot with lobster sauce to start, then lamb cutlets, compôte of pigeons and grilled mushrooms to follow, with a haunch of venison, boiled capon and oysters, pressed ox tongue and various vegetables and salads for the main course – not to mention the ices and puddings to follow afterwards. The kitchen would be hot as Hades, and Mrs Bragg in no mood for interruptions – not even from Rory Vye.

'I suppose you're right,' he admitted. 'If only the remains of your nursery supper had not looked quite so unappetising. Wait a minute! What about the delights of the still room? Perhaps Mrs Henderson can be persuaded to take pity on me – or even better, the lovely Iris. Now, back to bed this minute, you naughty children, or I shall have to tell your parents that you have led me astray.' And he rushed at those nearest to him with another ferocious roar, which sent them all skittering back into the room, screaming at the tops of their voices. Just as well the nursery was far enough away from the dining room to be out of earshot, I thought to myself.

'I'm *so* glad Rory's home,' Harriet said, watching her brother as he sauntered off down the corridor, straightening his tweed jacket. 'Now we shall have some fun! Don't look so disapproving, Polly. You must love Rory – everybody does.'

I was not quite sure what to think about Rory Vye, to be honest. He was a charmer all right, but he had made me feel uncomfortable and awkward. I thought he had a cheek, too, turning up so late and then expecting a meal to be specially prepared for him. Still, perhaps I was only being hard on him because of the mood I was in that evening. Looking at Miss Harriet's happy face, I decided to tell her what had happened some other time; there would be time enough the next day.

I saw Master Rory in the still room a little while later, eating jam out of the jar with a teaspoon and bothering Iris while she turned a chocolate bombe out of its mould. If Mrs Henderson had been there, I'm sure she would have dropped a few hints that he should leave, but she was upstairs checking the bedrooms. And then Iris noticed me walk past and came running out, wiping her hands on her apron.

'Oh, Polly! I've just heard what happened. What is to be done? Surely you cannot really be leaving!'

'I can, and I am,' I told her, biting my lip. 'And it is my own fault – I have no one to blame but myself.' As if that made my troubles any easier to bear.

SIX

I ask you whether one reason why disobedience is so common among young servants is because they do not see the beauty of obedience. On the contrary, they think it is 'spirited' to let folks see that they have got a will of their own. Oh, that I could but show you the ugliness of disobedience, how loathsome and hateful a thing it is when compared with the sweet beauty of obedience!

From *The Dignity of Service and Other Sermons Especially Addressed to Servants*, Revd Henry Housman, 1876

'I've an older sister who's a housekeeper up in London,' William said. 'Shall I ask her if she knows of a decent family in need of a housemaid? I'm sure she'll soon hear of something.'

'Oh, don't you go bothering her on my account. I shall probably find a place around here sooner or later.'

It was kind of William to put himself out for me and I

didn't want to sound ungrateful, but somehow I didn't fancy the idea of working in the city. Ada from our village had gone to London as a general servant for a grocer and his family. 'She's to slave away from five in the morning till gone midnight,' her mother reported after a week, 'with only a drunken cook and one lazy footman for company – and nothing but a few leftovers to eat!' No, I wanted to work in a big house with plenty of other girls to be friends with, and pleasant places to walk on my afternoons off, and good food on the table. Still, beggars can't be choosers. I had precious little chance of finding work in a place like Swallowcliffe again, with the character reference Mrs Henderson would give me.

William would not be put off. 'Let me have your address just in case, and I'll write to you if I hear anything,' he said. 'It's a small world, and who knows? We may well run into each other again. Here's hoping, Polly. I shall miss our early-morning talks.' And he looked at me quite seriously for a change.

'Cheer up! There'll be another girl for you to talk to soon enough,' I said, trying to make light of it. The truth was, I would miss him too – though I wasn't going to give him any ideas by saying as much – and didn't want to think that this might be the last time we would be speaking to each other. I could still hardly believe that my time at the Hall was coming to an end so soon. The ball was to be held that evening; most of our guests were going home the next day and I would be leaving with them.

That afternoon, we were given a couple of hours off before our work began in earnest, so Iris suggested we go for a walk around the lake. I would gladly have jumped into it by that time to get away from Jemima's gloating face – although the water was presently frozen over, what with the bitter cold weather we'd been having. Spiky trees stood out dark against a sky already streaked with pink, and little matchstick figures were gliding about over the clean, white ice. Miss Harriet was out skating with her brothers – I could hear her calling to one of them, and Master John laughing excitedly about something, which made me smile, and then Rory and Edward's deeper voices underneath.

I looked back at the house and pictured what was going on behind those quiet walls. The ladies would be upstairs, changing into fancy tea gowns, while William and the other footmen would be hurrying between the kitchen and the drawing room below with plates of crumpets and tea cakes, sponges and scones. Lamps glowed in the windows; soon Mrs Henderson would be doing her rounds, drawing curtains and closing shutters against the darkening winter afternoon. I had been part of this world for just a little while, and it would go on its merry way perfectly well without me.

I had still not had the chance to tell Harriet what had befallen me – nor the heart, either, because I knew how sorry she would be to see me go. I would explain the next day just before I left; there was no point in spoiling her fun now.

'Come and join us!' she called as we came nearer, and then skated over to where we stood. 'Margaret has gone in and left her skates behind. Look, by that tree trunk. You can take turns with them.'

'Not me,' Iris said, laughing and shaking her head. 'I could not skate if my life depended upon it.'

'Come on then, Polly!' Harriet coaxed. 'Don't disappoint me too. It is such fun!' And she twirled a graceful loop, her red tartan skirt flying out in a wide circle.

Why not? I thought to myself. Might as well be hanged for a sheep as a lamb; I could hardly be dismissed twice, anyway. So, without more ado, I sat on the tree trunk, took off my boots and laced up the skates, which were on the small side but not too uncomfortable. My friend Millie and I used to spend hours on the village pond when it froze over in winter: she had been passed down two pairs of skates from her twin brothers, which came in very handy for me. So out I sailed and, for a few glorious minutes, all my troubles went streaming away into the air behind me. There can be nothing better than skimming along, light as a feather, while the smooth ice rushes past under your feet and your lungs fill up with so much cold, clean air that you could almost spread out your arms and take off into the sky like some great wild bird.

'Wait for me!' Harriet called from somewhere far away, and I came to my senses to find myself right out in the middle of the lake. Slowly I skated back towards her, savouring every minute of my freedom. For one moment Swallowcliffe belonged to me. The lake and the trees and the sky above – even the house itself – were as much mine as they were anybody's, because I had become a part of them and they were a part of me. Perhaps I would not vanish into thin air when the time came to go but leave something of myself behind, just like Ignatius. The next girl to sleep in that bed under the window might wake up one morning with a dream of me in her head, even though she would not know where it had come from, or quite what it was. Listen to me talk! And yet somehow it was comforting to think so.

I held out my hand to Harriet and we took a turn around together, arm in arm. Master Rory had left the ice to talk to Iris, and Edward was skating over to join them – that only left Master John, who was making his way out to the middle of the lake, where I had just been. 'Not too far out!' I called to him. He could skate very well for a boy of his age, but I did not feel happy about him going so far away. The lake had been frozen only for a couple of days, and we did not know exactly how thick the ice was. I disentangled myself from Harriet and made my way over to bring him back. John was a great favourite in the house; he and Miss Harriet were allowed to take their supper with us in the servants' hall sometimes as a treat, and everyone was pleased to see them.

'Turn around now, Master John,' I called again, but he only looked back and laughed at me over his shoulder, thinking this was a great game. 'No, I mean it,' I shouted to him, quickening my pace and growing more worried by the minute. I did not want to chase him further out across the ice, but it was dangerous for him to be so far away. If anything happened, we should not be able to reach him quickly enough.

'John! Come here at once,' Harriet shouted behind me, but her little brother only skated faster.

And then my worst fears were suddenly realised, with a speed that took us all by surprise. There was a sudden crack that sounded like a gunshot across the quiet lake and the ice gave way under John's skates, shattering into pieces all around him. He disappeared, falling headlong into the darkness below. For a heart-stopping second we could see nothing. Then his head emerged and one frantic arm waved above the surface, trying to find something – anything – to hold on to in the treacherous sea of water and bobbing chunks of ice, and the sight of that despairing, sinking arm shocked us back to life.

'No!' Harriet screamed, starting to race towards him.

I grabbed her arm. 'Stop! Go much closer and the ice will give way under you too.'

'But we have to do something! Are we just going to stand there and watch him drown?'

'Take off your scarf and follow me,' I said, trying not to panic. My father had told me what to do if ever someone should fall through the ice: you were to get down flat on your stomach, to spread the weight evenly, and try to drag the person out with something like a rope, or even a tree branch. There was no rope to hand, but I had a shawl and Harriet a long woollen scarf – we would have to manage with that.

'John, we're coming to pull you out,' I shouted, skating as close as I dared and then dropping to my hands and knees. The ice groaned beneath me and I quickly fell flat on my stomach, spreading out my arms and legs. Fifteen feet or so from the boy was as near as I could get. I saw his desperate white face just above the inky water; we had seconds before the cold got to him and he disappeared under the surface.

Harriet was lying flat on the ice next to me. I grabbed her scarf and tied a knot in one end, then knotted my shawl to the other. 'Wriggle as close as you can and throw him this,' I ordered, pushing her in front; she was lighter than me. 'I'll hold your ankles and pull you both back.'

'Catch the scarf, Johnny,' she shouted, bunching it up in her hand. 'We'll get you out!'

Once, twice, three times she had to throw our makeshift rope out to her brother before he managed to grab hold of it and we could begin to haul him towards us. A wide corridor of ice gave way in his path, and I had to squirm frantically backwards or Harriet and I would have fallen through ourselves. I think we were both beginning to panic then. We could not tow the boy all the way back to the shore! He would have drowned before we reached it.

'Flip yourself up on the ice, John,' I called out to him. 'Just like a big fish! That's the way!'

At last he came to a layer of ice that was thick enough to bear his weight. With Harriet pulling as hard as she could, and me holding her legs to anchor them, John finally managed to roll himself out of the water on to the ice. He lay there, exhausted, still clutching the other end of the scarf for dear life. We reeled him in like that big fish he pretended to be, and then I took his limp, sodden body in my arms and skated for the shore as I had never skated before. Master Edward seized the boy from me, wrapped his coat around him and started running towards the house without another word.

'Is he alive?' Rory's eyes asked the question – I was not sure whether he had actually spoken.

'I think we got him out in time, Sir,' I said, through chattering teeth. Yet John's face was so white, bluish even around the lips, and I could still feel the deadly cold of his body seeping through my clothes. I had an awful feeling he had been in that icy water for too long.

'We saved him,' Harriet said, bursting into tears. I hoped to goodness she was right.

She gave me her skates to carry and then she and Rory ran on to the house behind Master Edward. Iris and I trudged behind. '*You* saved him,' she said to me. 'I saw what you did, and Mrs Henderson is going to hear about it too.'

'Oh, don't say anything,' I told her. 'I'm in enough trouble as it is.'

It was hard to go back to the house and carry on with our work as though nothing had happened, but Mrs Henderson would have had my guts for garters if she'd heard me talking to anyone. There was nothing for it but to put on our caps and aprons, for Iris to take up her place in the still room and for me to help the others set up the fifty or more little round tables in the dining and drawing rooms, each with its own silver candelabrum and bowl of flowers on the white linen tablecloth. Twenty extra footmen had been hired from London for the night, and a French chef had been busy in the kitchen with a team of maids since early that morning, preparing the refreshments. You can imagine what Mrs Bragg had to say about that! Her cooking was good enough for every day but not for fancy occasions, that's what she must have thought, and it didn't seem fair to me.

We had already washed the floor in the ballroom and given it a coat of beeswax and turpentine; now Mr Wilkins was sprinkling over a layer of French chalk so the dancers would not fall over themselves. The gardeners had been up the whole night, raking the lawns and the drive, and you could not move for flowers all over the house, everywhere you looked. There would be champagne for the guests first, and then they would have their dinner; the dancing would start at ten, stop at midnight for fireworks over the lake, and carry on till two in the morning when it was time for the hot breakfast with more champagne. There were enough bottles coming up from the cellar to keep the whole of the British navy afloat. My last night at Swallowcliffe would certainly be one to remember.

We must each have gone up and down those stairs fifty times. There were cans of hot water to be taken up for the hip baths, fires to be stoked, and however many towels did our guests get through? Both the huge linen closets on the landing were emptied; they would have to work till midnight in the laundry to have fresh supplies ready for the morning. We hurried to and fro with flowers and fans and evening jackets that suddenly needed pressing right that minute and another cup of tea for the Countess – oh, and could Lady Pemberley have a gardenia for her corsage, since those orchids were just the wrong shade of pink and clashed too horribly with her gown?

We gathered together in the servants' hall for a quick supper at seven, those of us who managed to get away. I could not stop thinking about poor Master John. How was he? His name had not been mentioned, which surely had to be a good sign. If the worst had happened or his life was in any danger, we would have been told to stop preparing for the ball, wouldn't we? But now Mrs Henderson was telling us each our duties. The conservatory had been turned into a dressing room for the ladies, and since I was not maiding for anyone in particular, I would be sitting there for most of the evening to offer any help that might be needed – after our house guests had come downstairs and we had cleaned up their bedrooms, of course.

'Not so fast,' the housekeeper said, as I curtseyed and prepared to leave. 'You're to come with me for a moment first.'

Oh, she did look cross! Somebody must have seen me out skating with Miss Harriet. I hurried along behind her as we made our way to the front of the house, wondering how I was going to explain that away, and why we were not going to her room for my dressing-down. Imagine how I felt when she opened the drawing-room door and beckoned me through with a nod of her head. Lady Vye was standing by the mantelpiece, and His Lordship sitting in a chair on the other side of it. They were both in evening dress. Lady Vye's gown was the most beautiful thing I had ever seen, deep blue shot through with green and with a long train like a shimmering peacock's tail. I had only a second to take it in, however; Mrs Henderson pushed me forward and I stood in front of them both, staring at the carpet.

'Henderson tells me you went out on the lake this afternoon,' Her Ladyship said.

'Yes, M'lady.' I could feel my knees start to tremble. What could she do to me now? I'd already been given notice to leave. Perhaps she was going to dock part of my wages for insolence; I should have found that very hard to take, on top of everything else.

'And I gather you were instrumental in getting John out of the water.'

'Yes, M'lady.' For a second, I forgot to keep looking down. 'How is he? Will he be all right?'

Mrs Henderson tutted in exasperation and gave me a sharp nudge in the back.

'Sorry, M'lady.' I dropped my eyes immediately, hoping my bad manners would be excused in the heat of the moment.

'He has had quite a shock but the doctor assures us there will be no lasting ill effects,' she replied. There was a pause. 'If you had not acted so quickly, it might have been a different matter.'

Thank goodness for that. I could not help smiling from the relief, and had to curtsey hurriedly because that was probably disrespectful too.

'We are very grateful to you,' Lord Vye said.

You could have knocked me down with a feather! All I knew of His Lordship was a solemn voice at morning prayers and a distant figure in the corridor that would send us scattering for cover; we knew he hated to be disturbed going about his business. Becky had told me she had even hidden in a cupboard once, hearing his step outside the room and not having any other means of escape. And now here he was, smiling at me! Something about his expression reminded me of my father – which is the only time a viscount has been compared to a fisherman, I should imagine. That was certainly a thought to keep to myself.

Then Lady Vye cut in, and that was the next extraordinary thing. 'I have discussed the matter with Henderson,' she said, 'and decided to give you another chance. There were aspects of your behaviour that I found quite unacceptable, but clearly your heart is in the right place. Henderson tells me your work is satisfactory on the whole and you are still young – there is hope you will improve. You may continue to work at the Hall, so long as you manage to control your conduct. Do you understand? There is no place for a saucy, bold little madam here.'

'Yes, M'lady. No, M'lady,' I stammered, feeling as though I could have jumped for joy! However that would have done me no good at all, so I merely curtseyed again so deeply that I nearly fell over.

'That is all,' she said. 'Off you go.'

'Just a minute.' His Lordship was beckoning me towards him. Oh Lord, he wasn't going to disagree with her, was he? No, he reached into his pocket and then slipped something into my hand. It was a sovereign – a whole gold sovereign! I had to look twice at the coin before I realised what it was, never having seen one before.

'Good girl,' he said, and smiled at me again. 'You did well today.'

SEVEN

I hurried back to work up the servants' staircase as though I were floating on air. My job back, and a sovereign into the bargain! Never in my wildest dreams had I expected such a stroke of luck. All along the upstairs landing, bedroom doors were opening and the ladies came sailing out in rustling clouds of silk and taffeta, chiffon and ostrich feathers. Some were already wearing their masks, others fluttered fans before their faces. The air seemed to hum with excitement, laughter and whispered secrets. Miss Eugenie was the belle of the ball, very grown-up and elegant in ivory *crêpe de chine* embroidered all over with seed pearls and a mask in her hand made of swans' feathers. I hoped the evening would be everything she could have wanted, and more.

'You look pleased with yourself all of a sudden,' Jemima remarked as we started to tidy up the bedrooms.

'I am not to leave after all,' I told her, brushing up a quantity of face powder which the Duchess had managed to spill over the carpet. She had made a proper mess. 'They have given me another chance.'

That took the wind out of Jemima's sails. 'Better not waste it, then,' she remarked. 'You must have used up all of your nine lives by now.' I could tell she was put out but I did not take any notice. Nothing could spoil my mood that night.

When the rooms were back in their proper order and the slops at last emptied away, I went to take my place in the conservatory dressing room. It had been set up with several dressing tables and a full-length cheval mirror, and the ladies soon started trickling in: dropping off cloaks and furs for me to hang up, checking their reflections or adjusting their hair. Once the dancing began at ten, I was not so busy – until a very grand lady in burgundy brocade came sweeping through the door.

'Can you sew tolerably well?' she asked me.

'Yes, ma'am. At least, so I have been told.'

'Good,' she said, settling down in a chair. 'I have had the misfortune to dance with the clumsiest man in Christendom, and the wretched fellow put his foot on my gown and ripped off half the hem. Just take a look! Can you do anything with it?'

'I think so, ma'am,' I said, inspecting the damage. It was a long tear, but luckily just above the black lace trim, so my stitches would be hidden. 'I'll do my best, anyway.'

'If you're quick about it, you shall have a shilling.' She fanned herself vigorously. 'What a thing to happen! And a new gown, too. My dressmaker only finished it yesterday.'

I had been provided with a sewing box in case of just such an emergency, so I knelt beside her on the floor and began stitching away. It was very quiet and peaceful and I was beginning to think she might have nodded off, when in came another lady who was evidently an old friend of hers and looked much the same sort of person, only not quite so stout. They fell to talking straight away in the kind of easy tones people take when they are well-acquainted. I could not help but overhear, although at first the gossip meant little to me as I did not know the names that were mentioned. But then the talk turned to the Vye family, and my ears pricked up.

'That Eugenie's a pretty little thing,' my large lady said. 'No wonder Clara wants her married off in a hurry and out of the way – far too much competition.' She was evidently not a great admirer of Lady Vye.

Her friend leaned forward and lowered her voice confidentially, although there were no other ladies in the room at the time. 'They had better hope she makes a good match. You'd never think so to judge from this evening, but I've heard that somebody needs to bring some money into the family. Nobody can make a living out of farming these days, and a place like Swallowcliffe must cost a fortune to run.'

'My dear, there's talk they may have to sell off part of the estate. Really, it's a disgrace! Our finest houses are all being bought up by bankers and factory owners, and who knows what state England will be in by the end of the century.'

There was a pause while they both fanned themselves. 'There's always Edward, I suppose,' said the other lady eventually. I could tell she was rather put out to find herself the bearer of stale news. 'Perhaps he can catch one of these rich American girls who seem to be all the rage in London. There's bound to be a new batch coming over for the season. Some of them are perfectly lovely, I hear, and with better manners than one might imagine.'

The conversation turned to more general matters, and shortly afterwards I came to the end of my sewing. I snipped off the thread and got up, my legs half asleep from having been in the same position for so long.

'Oh! I had quite forgotten you were there,' my lady said, rather taken aback. 'You're a quiet one, aren't you?' She glanced down at the hem of her gown and then opened the beaded evening bag hanging from her elbow. 'I think I shall only give you sixpence, since you have taken such a time.'

I might have said that it was a very long tear and she ought to have given me twice as much as she'd promised for mending it, rather than half, but as a matter of fact I did not. After all, there was a sovereign in my pocket. I did not feel sorry to see those ladies go, and wished I had not had to listen to them talk in that way; it was a worry to think of the Vyes being short of money.

I went to check the bedrooms upstairs, my head spinning with all kinds of thoughts I didn't know what to do with. What a strange evening it was turning out to be, and shortly to become stranger still. I bumped into a lady on our servants' staircase; she must have lost her way, although I didn't see how she could have gone so far astray as to end up there. I curtseyed and stood aside to let her pass, wondering whether it would be rude to offer her directions back to the ballroom. She was wearing a lovely pale green gown, with a white pierrot mask over her face.

And then I had my second shock of the evening. 'Polly? It's me!' came a familiar voice, and the mask was snatched away to reveal—

'Iris?'

I stood there staring at her, lost for words. 'What are you doing?' I managed to gasp eventually. 'Where has that dress come from? And the mask? What if Mrs Henderson sees you?'

'She won't know who I am. You wouldn't have, would you, unless I'd decided to take it off? I couldn't resist giving you a surprise.'

I could not stop looking at Iris. She was the equal of anyone in that ballroom and finer than most, with her beautiful eyes shining and such a mischievous grin on her face that you could not help but smile back at her. I lifted a ruffle on her dress, feeling the silk cool and smooth against my fingers. 'Wherever did you get this?'

'It's an old one of the mistress's in my last place. I was keeping it for our servants' ball.' Her face changed and she added quickly, 'I'm sorry. You won't want to hear about that.'

'No, it's all right,' I reassured her. 'I was going to tell you – Lady Vye's changed her mind, after what happened with

Master John. I am not to be dismissed after all.'

'Quite right too! I knew Mrs Henderson would speak up for you.'

'Have a care, Iris,' I warned. 'She's bound to notice if you're away too long.'

'Don't worry, I am only going for the one dance. She won't even know I've gone.' She slipped past me on the stairs, then turned back with one last dazzling smile. 'There's a gentleman waiting for me, Polly. I can't let him down – not after he has gone to the trouble of finding me a mask and these lovely gloves.' She stretched out both arms to show me the swankiest pair of white kid gloves, right up to the elbow. Oh, she did look a picture! I'd have given my eye teeth for some gloves like that, with my hands being so rough and chapped from hard work.

'Wish me luck, Polly,' she said, before the mask went on again and she had turned back into a stranger.

'Good luck, then,' I said, but she had already disappeared.

I went on my way upstairs, more worried than ever. Iris was bound to have admirers, being so pretty, but she was playing a dangerous game if there was a gentleman involved. The stakes were high, and she had a lot to lose. Trying to pass herself off as a lady would land her in a great deal of trouble, I thought, even if she got away with it so far as Mrs Henderson was concerned. Real life wasn't like those romantic novelettes Iris was so fond of reading, where the master of the house would end up marrying the governess, or the scullery maid would turn out to be the long-lost daughter of a duke, who happened to recognise her when she was throwing out the pigswill. (She had lent me one of them once, but I couldn't get anywhere with it.) Gentlemen weren't in the habit of marrying maidservants, so far as I knew, no matter how beautiful they were.

I don't think any of us servants went to bed that night. By the time supper had been cleared away, we had to start preparing tables for the hot breakfast at three in the morning: devilled kidneys, rump steak with oyster sauce, roast partridges and lamb cutlets. And by the time *that* had been cleared away, some of the guests who had gone to bed at a reasonable time were getting up; they needed fires made up in their rooms, and hot water to wash, and then another ordinary breakfast as usual. Even with the extra footmen, we were rushed off our feet. I only saw Iris for a moment again – back in her black uniform and apparently no one but me and her gentleman friend any the wiser about what she had been up to.

At seven in the morning, we all sat down in the servants' hall for our own breakfast, half dropping with tiredness but in one mind that the ball could be declared a great success. Eugenie had looked lovely and danced all night,

Master Rory's cavalry officer friends had charmed all the ladies and been as dashing as anyone could have wished, and the food was very splendid, by all accounts – although we still thought Mrs Bragg was as fine a cook as the French chef, for all his airs and graces. At least the day ahead would be fairly quiet: most of our guests were leaving in the afternoon, and then the whole family was going to a neighbour's for dinner.

By the evening, the tables had been cleared away, the footmen had gone back to London, our guests had departed, their bedrooms were stripped and aired, and the house settled back into itself. Master Edward and Master Rory were staying on for a while longer, but that did not mean too much extra work for us. I did not have a chance to be with Iris privately over the next few days, but I watched her. She kept herself to herself and at last I realised she did not want to confide in me; she could have found an occasion, had she wanted to. That hurt me a little, I must admit. I had thought we were closer friends than that. Perhaps she thought I was too young to understand about love and romance – although she used to tease me about William, calling him my 'young man' just to see me blush. He and I were friendly, that was all, although he did seem very pleased to hear that I would be staying on at the Hall. He had told me that he had a younger sister, of whom he was very fond, and I probably reminded him of her. If anything, I thought he might have been keen on Iris; he was always the first to notice if she was struggling to carry anything heavy, and the three of us had once spent a very pleasant afternoon together, after we'd come across him on one of our Sunday walks.

Anyone could tell that something was afoot with Iris. You could see how happy she was just by looking at her face, and I was not the only one to notice. 'Why are you so full of the joys of spring?' Becky asked one morning, hearing her singing to herself as she brushed her hair, but she only shrugged the question off with a smile.

I badly wanted to warn her again to be careful, although I knew she wouldn't thank me for it. You see, the suspicion was growing on me that the gentleman who was paying her so much attention could only be Rory Vye. All his cavalry officer friends had left the house by now, and Master Edward was hardly the type to flirt with a maid. I thought back to that first evening when I had seen Master Rory in the still room, and then how eager Iris had been to watch him skating on the lake, and how quickly he had left the ice to talk to her. I knew very little about gentlemen and how they went about their business, but it was obvious that Rory was the type to break hearts. He could not help charming everyone, it was in his nature; if Iris took him at his word, she was bound to be disappointed.

Almost a week after the ball, I was woken up in the

middle of the night by the screech of a fox outside, and it barked several times again to make sure that I stayed awake. I lifted my head off the pillow to see whether anyone else had been disturbed by the eerie noise – and then sat up in bed to rub my eyes and look again. No, I had not been mistaken: Iris's bed was empty.

Where could she have been? With chamber pots under each bed, we had no reason to wander about and Mrs Henderson would have had plenty to say about it had she caught one of us! What did Iris think she was doing, out on her own somewhere in the middle of the night? Then I drew back the thin curtain to look out of the window, and what I saw only added to my fears. A full moon hung low in the sky, and its light revealed a figure hurrying along the shadowy path by the edge of the lake: a woman in a black cloak with some sort of pale dress underneath. I knew immediately this had to be Iris. She was alone, but somebody was obviously expecting her in the boathouse. A fire had been lit in the grate: I could see smoke rising from the chimney, and the flash of a white shirt at the window. A man was waiting for her there in the dark – and I had a good idea who that man might be.

EIGHT

A remark lately made to me by a friend of mine, mistress of a small household, often recurs to my mind. It struck me as so exactly expressing what was needed. 'Ellen', she said, 'was at one time rather given to flirtation, but I steered her through it.' Now that seems to me exactly what we should do, 'steer them through it'.

From *Our Responsibilities and Difficulties as Mistresses of Young Servants,* Lady Baker, 1886

I tried my best to stay awake until Iris came back, but my bed was too warm and snug and me too tired upon it to keep my eyes open for long. Before I knew what had happened, Mary was calling for us to wake up. Perhaps it took Iris a little longer than usual to rouse herself; I might have been imagining things, given what I thought I had seen in the night. I watched her intently, but her face gave nothing away. No one would have thought anything was out of the ordinary as she quickly washed, slipped into her print dress and brushed out her thick fair hair before plaiting it to pin up under a cap. Then off she went as usual to bring Mrs Henderson her early-morning cup of tea.

There was never a second to spare as our day began, but I had to try and find out whether my eyes had been playing tricks on me. Perhaps there was some clue among Iris's things as to what she might have been up to. I casually picked up her hairbrush as if to borrow it, and noticed a small damp leaf, caught between the bristles. Not definite proof, perhaps, but enough to make me determined to look for more evidence later on, when I was cleaning the room. When I saw traces of fresh mud on Iris's outdoor boots under the bed and felt the sodden hem of her coat, hanging behind the door, I knew for sure: she *was* that girl I had seen out by the lake. Well, that was a shock, although I didn't know what to do about it. Iris wasn't interested in my advice – she had made that clear enough. She ought to be more careful, though. What if it had been Mrs Henderson watching her out of the window, rather than me?

When we heard a few days later that Master Rory was finally going back to his barracks in London, I breathed a huge sigh of relief. At least now I could fall asleep without worrying what Iris might be up to. I hoped that he would be away for a good long time, and that she would have come to her senses by the next time he paid us a visit. Master Edward was staying on at Swallowcliffe a little longer, but he spent most of the time reading up in his room and was not much trouble to anyone – apart from a rather inconvenient interest in photography, that is. He had bought a wooden box camera in Oxford and used to wander around the house with it, getting in everyone's way. We would have to stop what we were doing and stand without moving a muscle for ten or fifteen minutes at a time while he disappeared under a cloth at the back, fiddling about with goodness knows what levers and switches. It got so bad we used to run away and hide if we saw him coming, but poor Iris was a sitting target in the still room and found it less easy to escape. Still, it was a fairly harmless occupation, I suppose; at least he didn't make much of a mess.

Two things happened shortly after Master Edward left too which changed my life a great deal for the better. The first was that finally our third housemaid arrived; I made up a pair with her, and Jemima went back to working with Becky. The new maid's name was Amelia, but Mrs Henderson soon decided that was much too fancy a name for such a position and that she should be known as Jane instead, the same as the girl before. As soon as I saw Amelia/Jane, I thought we should probably get along together perfectly well, and so it turned out. She was a quiet, steady sort of girl who worked hard and only spoke when she had good reason to: a blessed relief after having to cope with all Jemima's flouncing about. The two of us soon found our own rhythm and made a very efficient pair, if I do say so myself. Just as well, because the Vyes would shortly be going up to London for the season (Miss Eugenie was to be presented at Court, to complete her coming out), and we would be starting on the spring cleaning when the weather had warmed up a little.

Then came the second piece of good news. Jemima had been chosen to go up to London with the family and work as parlourmaid in the townhouse there for the season. That was a feather in her cap and no mistake; she went about looking very pleased with herself.

'One way to wriggle out of the spring cleaning, I suppose,' Mary remarked, but I did not mind in the slightest. She would be away until July or August at least, and that could only be another relief.

And then just to fill my cup of happiness to the brim, I learned that we were to be given Mothering Sunday as a holiday before the spring cleaning began, and could go home to visit our families! I could hardly wait, and counted off the days as February turned to March in an agony of impatience. Iris's people were miles away up in Yorkshire so I invited her to come with me; Mother would not mind, and it would be nice to have some company on the journey.

At last the great day came. The second coachman took we four maids off in the barouche to the railway station at Edenvale, about four miles away. Becky and Jane were going up to their families in South London, while Iris and I would go several stops down the line in the other direction to my village of Little Rising, where Mother would be waiting to meet us. I was wearing an old blouse and skirt of Miss Eugenie's which Harriet had begged for me, since they would be quite out of fashion by the time they fitted her, and in the basket on my lap was a pair of stout boots for my little brother Tom, hardly worn, together with two of Harriet's outgrown cotton frocks and a thick woollen coat which my sister Lizzie could wear next winter. Mrs Henderson had let us bake simnel cakes in the still room range to take home and delicious smells were wafting up from my basket where the cake lay on top of the clothes, wrapped up in greaseproof paper.

It was a fine day, so we had the hood folded back to look at the countryside as we trotted smartly through it – and to give poor Iris some air, as she was feeling rather queasy from the bucketing motion of the carriage. Everywhere was lush and green after all the rain we had been having; the trees and hedgerows were heavy with blossom or dotted with tightly-furled emerald buds on every branch, so fat you could almost feel them straining to burst open. Lambs frisked about in the fields, wagging their little woolly tails, rabbits scuttered away into the long grass before our wheels, and a springtime promise of new life blew towards us on the breeze. The birds were singing their hearts out, the sun was shining, and if I had been any happier I would have burst too.

Becky smiled at me across the carriage. I must say, she was a great deal more pleasant to the rest of us when Jemima was not around. When we arrived at the station to find that there was a half hour to wait before either train arrived, she rummaged in her bag and took out a letter she had received from Jemima in London the week before which we could read to pass the time.

18 March, 1890

My dear Rebecca,

Well, I am thoroughly ashamed for taking so long to write to you! The truth is, I have had scarcely a minute to myself since we arrived in Eaton Square. We have had quite a stream of visitors. All of London society seems to have come knocking at our door — no doubt to see Miss Eugenie, who must be one of the prettiest girls out this season. If you could only have seen her in the gown she wore to be presented at Court . . .

Lord and Lady Vye have been invited to several balls at Buckingham Palace and apparently Her Ladyship is becoming quite a favourite with the Prince of Wales. I should think he might well be invited to shoot at Swallowcliffe come the autumn, and won't that send Mrs Bragg into a state! We have guests to supper nearly every night – not to mention trips to the opera and the theatre, and endless card parties. Of course this means late nights for me also, but I have a fair-sized room to myself and am often able to rest there in the early afternoon, so I do not mind. These tall white houses in Eaton Square are delightful, far more convenient and modern than a rambling old place like Swallowcliffe, and so much easier to clean.

Turning to more interesting matters: I must tell you about another of our visitors of whom you may eventually come to hear yourself. She is a young American lady by the name of Kate Brookfield, over here with her mother on a tour of Europe. Lady Vye has been taking particular pains to cultivate their friendship, and I should not be at all surprised to see Miss Brookfield at Swallowcliffe too one day – and maybe as something more than a guest! She is quite beautiful and heiress to a great fortune, so of course she would make a wonderful *match for Master Edward. He was down from Oxford last weekend to stay with the family and seemed very struck by her. Miss Brookfield is an accomplished horsewoman so they have been out riding together in the park with Lady Vye, and Master Rory too, whose barracks are nearby. Who knows how things may turn out?*

There is no need to ask you for news of Swallowcliffe, because I am sure everything will have been going on much the same! I must admit, life in the country is bound to seem rather dull after the excitement of London, but perhaps I will be ready for a rest by then. At any rate it will be very nice to see you again; I can tell you everything else I am too tired to write now.

With fondest affection,
Jemima Newgate

The letter made me smile – Jemima's voice came through so very clearly – although Iris seemed rather put out after she had finished reading. It was easy enough to guess the reason why: she would not have liked to think of Master Rory riding about with a beautiful American heiress. By the time our train came, however, she had managed to recover her spirits and we spent the rest of the journey chatting away like nobody's business. That day, I felt as though my good friend Iris had come back to me, and very glad I was to find her again.

She told me a little about her childhood and her parents, who were both quite elderly and lived in a three-storey terraced house on the outskirts of York. Being Baptists, they had brought up Iris and her two older sisters in a strict, God-fearing household; one which – from what I could make out – did not have a great deal of love or laughter in it. I worried for a moment that Iris might think our cottage very shabby and poor compared to her home, but there was nothing to be done about that now. Before I knew it, we were pulling into the station, and there were my sisters and brother running alongside the train down the platform, and my darling mother waiting to greet us.

'Why, Polly,' she said, holding me at arms' length for a moment, 'just look at you! You are properly grown up!'

I had been gone less than three months, and yet I truly did feel like a different person – both inside and out. So much had happened to me since I had arrived at Swallowcliffe, and I suppose Eugenie's fine clothes made me seem older too. Mother was almost shy with me at first, particularly in front of Iris, who could not help putting everyone else in the shade on account of her looks. She was even more lovely than usual in her Sunday best, if still a little pale from the see-saw carriage ride, and my younger sister Martha took to her immediately. I

don't think she let go of Iris's hand the entire visit, apart from when we were sitting down to eat. Luckily my other sister Lizzie can talk the hind leg off a donkey, which gave the rest of us time to get used to each other. Iris gave my mother the sunshine yellow flowers she had picked that morning — daffodils, marsh marigolds and colt's foot, wrapped up in damp moss and tied with ivy. Tom held her other hand and mine in his own, demanding to be swung between us, and by the time we were half a mile down the road for home, everyone felt quite comfortable in each other's company.

I could hardly believe how tiny our cottage seemed to me now, after Swallowcliffe's large rooms and high ceilings; we could not all fit in the front room together. Perhaps that was just as well, though, since the kitchen was much warmer and more welcoming. Pots of red geraniums stood in a row along the windowsill, the whitewashed walls were bright and clean, and a colourful rag rug lay on the stone floor. Iris sat at the table with Martha on her lap, perfectly content, and I knew there was no reason to worry. Our house might have been poor, but I did not need to feel ashamed of it.

While the water was boiling for tea, Mother told me a piece of sad news: Reverend Conway had died unexpectedly a couple of weeks before. His daughter had already left the village to act as lady's companion to an elderly widow some twenty miles away, because a new vicar and his wife would shortly be arriving to take over the vicarage. I was sorry not to have been able to say goodbye, but Mother gave me Miss Conway's address so that I could write and wish her well. Then it was time for church, with a visiting curate in the pulpit instead of Reverend Conway (which seemed quite wrong to me), and the neighbours to greet afterwards. My mother has never been one to puff herself up, but she couldn't help looking proud of me. After the service we went home for slices of boiled bacon on toast, and then we all rambled through the fields down to the river while Iris and I told Mother about our lives at Swallowcliffe.

'Now you listen for a change, young Lizzie,' she said to my sister. 'If you can do half as well for yourself as our Polly has, I shall die a happy woman.'

It was lovely to be home! I hated saying goodbye at the end of the day, but I'd be coming back in the summer for a whole week which cheered me up a little. I had given my mother almost three pounds (including Lord Vye's sovereign); Tom was so pleased with his new boots he would probably be sleeping in them, and the same with Lizzie and her dresses – Martha even managed not to be jealous since she knew they would be coming to her in the end. It had been a lovely day, all in all, made perfect by the fact that Iris and I had shared it together. Now we were going back to the Hall to start on the spring cleaning, summer was on its way and, with a bit of luck, she would soon forget about Rory Vye.

NINE

What a great deal of work spring cleaning is! I soon began to feel that I knew every inch of Swallowcliffe Hall, from top to bottom, and every single thing under its roof. Mr Wilkins and William (who had been left behind to help us while Mr Goddard and the other two footmen went to London) brought out huge ladders from the stables and held them steady for us while we took down all the curtains in the house and unhooked the bed hangings. While the family was away, at least there was no need for them to wear livery; William spent most of his time in a waistcoat and shirt sleeves, that thick brown hair of his curling down over his collar. He did look handsome. Just as well we were so busy and that he was probably sweet on Iris anyway, or I might have been quite distracted.

We covered everything with dustcloths before the chimney sweeps came, then Mary and Mrs Henderson put away the ornaments (including one particular figurine with a spider's web of cracks all over it that was only too familiar to me), and we washed down the furniture with vinegar and scoured it with fine sand before a new layer of beeswax could be applied.

'Rub until the wood is warm!' Mrs Henderson ordered, so we polished away obediently until our arms ached. The carpets were taken up and dragged outside for the gardeners to hang over a clothes' line and beat as hard as they could, and all the wooden paintwork was scrubbed. Every speck of dust and soot from the countless fires that had burned over that long winter was sent flying, and we threw open the windows to let fresh spring air come flooding through the house.

We might have worked hard, but it was a happy time. With most of the upper servants away, the atmosphere in the servants' hall became a great deal more free and easy. Mrs Henderson mostly ate in her room, and Mary and Mr Wilkins did not mind us chatting at meal times – as long as we were careful not to gossip in front of them. Because Mrs Bragg was not there to cook for us, we were being paid board wages: a little extra to make up for not having proper meals. But Iris was still baking bread and rolls for the household, there were lettuces and tomatoes fresh from the greenhouse, butter and cheese in the dairy, and the butcher called three times a week so we could buy ham and sausages. We did not suffer over-much, and I was delighted to think of the extra money I could pass on to my mother.

The other wonderful thing was that a new piano had been ordered for Miss Eugenie, and Lady Vye sent word from London that the old one could be taken down to the servants' hall for our entertainment. It turned out that Mr Wilkins could play very well, and we had some merry sing-songs in the evening. Miss Harriet and Master John took to having their supper with us and then staying on for a while afterwards to join in. Master John had become particularly special to me since his accident (what a long time ago that seemed now!) and he seemed to pay extra attention to me in return. He would often come and sit on my lap, which made me feel very comfortable and motherly.

Things would have been perfect – if only I hadn't been so worried about Iris. She seemed to become sadder and more withdrawn as the weeks went by; as though she had retreated inside herself to a place where I couldn't follow.

'Come for a walk with me,' I coaxed her one Sunday afternoon. 'There are still a few bluebells left in the woods, and Miss Harriet says the swallows are here. Let's go down to the lake and see them!'

But she only shook her head and turned back to her book. 'You go, Polly. I'm not up to much today.'

Iris hadn't been up to much for some time, I thought. She didn't want to go anywhere or do anything, and the sad fact of the matter was, we were drifting apart. It's hard to stay close to someone when there's a secret wedged between you like a rock, no matter how hard you try to pretend it's not there. How could I help her if she wouldn't talk to me?

There was one time when I thought Iris came close to opening up to me. Once the spring cleaning was over, there was not much to do around the house until the family came back, so Mrs Henderson told me to work with Iris in the still room, making marmalade. The gardeners had brought in baskets full of plump, sour oranges from the hothouse; every one of them had to be peeled, and then the rind boiled for a good two hours and cut into tiny chips before being boiled up again with the fruit pulp and sugar syrup. A tall white sugar cone sat on the table, hard as marble, which we would have to break into chunks.

We had been talking about Miss Eugenie, who was apparently being courted by the Duke of Cheveny's older son, the Earl of Hitchingham – or so Becky had heard from Jemima. Iris told me that she didn't think much of this young man. When he had visited Swallowcliffe with his parents the previous autumn (they only lived in the next county), he had followed her down a passage and tried to kiss her. 'He had his hands all over me too,' she added, laying down the nippers. 'Ugh! It was horrible.'

I was shocked to hear it. 'Whatever did you do?'

'I pushed him away, good and hard, and told him I'd scream the house down if he didn't leave me alone. That frightened him off pretty quick, I can tell you.'

'But we should let Miss Eugenie know what he's like! What if he ended up proposing to her?'

Iris smiled, rather sadly. 'Do you think anyone would believe me if I told them what happened? The whole thing would end up being my fault, you can be sure of that. They'd say I led him on and then made a fuss when he took me at my word.' She started to attack the sugar cone again. 'Anyway, just because he did that to me, doesn't mean he'll treat Miss Eugenie the same way. Some of these gentlemen will try things on with a maid that they wouldn't dream of doing to a lady. You get the odd one who'll treat us both the same, but they're few and far between.'

She hesitated and I wondered whether she was about to say something else, but then she only sighed and laid down the nippers, and the moment was gone. 'This thing's as hard as a rock. We shall have to take the meat cleaver to it.'

That was quite a performance. Fragments of sugar ended up flying all over the place, but at last we had enough broken off to make up the syrup. 'Miss Eugenie will probably do all right for herself,' Iris said, wiping her hands on her apron. 'She'll end up the mistress of some big fancy house with lots of girls like us, no doubt, to keep it clean and comfortable. I wouldn't mind being in her shoes and neither would you, I should imagine.'

I wasn't so sure about that. Of course it would be lovely to wake up in a nice warm room, with a fire blazing away in the grate, but I'd sooner look after myself than ask somebody else to do it for me; that's how I was raised. Besides, whatever would I do all day, with nothing to keep my hands busy? Look at Miss Harriet: she was bored to death half the time, even though the new governess had arrived. She couldn't give two pins about those things that Eugenie was so good at: French and embroidery and poetry, and tinkling away on the piano.

'Don't go worrying about Miss Eugenie,' Iris told me, when the marmalade was bubbling away on the stove. 'There's no need to take the cares of the world on your shoulders. Just you look out for yourself, Polly – nobody else will.'

She was probably right, I thought, taking a deep breath of that sour, bitter-sweet tang of oranges and hot sugar which was to stay in our clothes and hair for days afterwards.

Because Iris was so preoccupied, I found myself spending more time with Miss Harriet. Things would have to change when the family came back, but in the meantime, nobody seemed to mind us going about together on my afternoon off or in the evenings, now that they were drawing out. She showed me all sorts of mysterious corners in the house that I'd never have found on my own: a part of the attic which was full of old furniture and chests of musty clothes; the tiny cell behind a wall in the drawing room, where a priest had once hidden when Henry VIII's soldiers came looking for Catholics; false shelves of books in the library which opened up to reveal a narrow, twisting staircase.

One sunny June afternoon, Miss Harriet and I climbed out on to the roof through a sash window in the corridor opposite our maids' bedroom. Harriet followed me along a narrow walkway between two chimney stacks and we came out on a flat part of the roof, like a square courtyard looking up to the blue sky above. It was quite safe, being shut in by more chimney stacks and a balustrade which ran all around the edge of the roof, and so private – just the place to talk. The weather had turned very warm at the beginning of the month, so we maids would sometimes sit out there at night for an hour or so when it was too hot to sleep in the attic room, whispering together so Mrs Henderson wouldn't hear us. I was glad to have a special place of my own to show Miss Harriet, in return for everywhere she'd taken me. Besides, I had been wanting to persuade her to take more account of her new governess; now was the perfect time to do it.

Miss Habershon, that was the governess's name, and she interested me a great deal. She was small and neat, with straight brown hair drawn back in a knot at the nape of her neck, and dressed all in black like an old crow, with not a scrap of lace or trimming to be seen. 'Well, no chance of His Lordship being led astray by *that* one,' Becky commented when we first saw Miss Habershon, and her appearance did take some getting used to – especially in one so young, for she couldn't have been more than twenty. After a while, though, I began to think that dressing so plainly quite suited her: you looked at her face, not her clothes, and then you noticed her pearly skin and clever dark eyes, drinking everything in.

She once came across me looking at a book from one of her shelves when I was meant to be dusting the room, but she didn't seem to mind. She told me I could take it away to read if I liked (which I did, having always been a great reader at school), and that I could borrow another one when I'd finished. It was a story by Charles Dickens called

Great Expectations, which I thought sounded very interesting – having some expectations of my own – and it must have had a great deal more to it than Iris's novelettes, because I couldn't go to sleep without reading a few pages every night, and had to beg another candle from Jane to finish it. So I was very kindly disposed towards Miss Habershon, and thought Miss Harriet should have paid her more attention.

'She knows about all sorts of things,' I said, once we were comfortably settled against a chimneystack on the roof. 'You should see the piles of books in her room – and there's a microscope. She has one of those new bicycles, too. Perhaps she could teach you to ride it.'

'She shouldn't even be there!' Harriet glowered. 'It's Nanny Roberts' room, not hers. I don't want anything to do with her, or her microscope, or her precious bicycle. She looks ridiculous on it, anyway. The gardeners were all laughing at her yesterday.'

I could tell it was time to hold my tongue, though I was disappointed Miss Harriet should think that way. 'Anyway, Rory and Edward will be home next month for my birthday,' she said, holding her face up to the sun. 'There'll be no time for lessons then.'

The family were probably ready for a break in the countryside, although the London season was still in full swing. Who wants to be stuck in a hot, noisy city in the middle of summer, when you could be paddling in a cool stream or walking in the shade of a wood? There would be some other guests from London coming down a little later too, including – and this was most exciting of all – the young American lady, Miss Brookfield, and her mother, who had another month in England before leaving for a tour of Italy. We had a good chat about that in the servants' hall, as you can imagine. I wanted to learn as much as I could about Miss Brookfield, because Mrs Henderson had told me that I was to act as her maid for the visit (Mary, Becky and Jane all being occupied with the married ladies). Apart from Miss Harriet, I had never maided for anyone before, and was feeling quite nervous about it. What if Miss Brookfield realised how young and inexperienced I was? What if I could not manage her hair?

The Vyes finally arrived back at Swallowcliffe, along with the staff who had been looking after them in London – Mrs Bragg and Mr Goddard, Jemima and Lord Vye's valet, the other footmen and the kitchenmaids. The rest of us stood in a circle on the front steps to welcome them home, along with Miss Harriet and Master John. Lady Vye certainly looked pleased to see her little boy; after all, she had been away from him for nearly four months. I shouldn't have liked to be separated from my own son for so long, but there you are – some things about the gentry I'll never understand. They had a few days to settle back into the house before Master Edward came down from Oxford and Master Rory from London, together with the Brockfields and our other guests.

I looked anxiously out of the window when the carriage that had gone to meet the new arrivals pulled in from the station, but the only glimpse of my lady was the sweep of a wide-brimmed hat and the swish of a lavender gown beneath, reaching out to take William's arm. So I tapped on the door of the Chinese Room without knowing quite what to expect, once Miss Brookfield and her luggage had been taken upstairs.

In a second, it opened wide and there she stood. Well, she was certainly beautiful, with greeny-grey eyes and copper-coloured hair that glinted in the sun like a new penny, but that was only the half of it. She spoke with a sort of lilting drawl that you could have listened to for hours, and had such a natural, easy manner about her that I knew right away she'd be a pleasure to work for. After I had told her who I was, she took me into the room and sat me down on the bed beside her. (I couldn't imagine Lady Vye ever doing that!)

'Now, Polly,' she said, smiling at me as though we had known each other for years, 'I am relying on you to tell me the drill around here. You must stop me making some awful mistake like wearing tweeds to dinner or insulting an important duchess. Will you be my helpmate, and try not to laugh if I say anything too stupid? I shall be quite lost otherwise, and people will say we Americans don't have the first idea how to behave.'

'I'm sure you don't need my advice, Miss,' I said, feeling myself blush with pleasure.

'Oh, but I do.' She laughed, jumping up. 'And you look so sweet and patient I know you will give it freely. Now, must I change for luncheon? And if so, which of these dresses should I choose?'

She flung open several of her suitcases and pulled out one gown after another until the bed was covered in a rainbow of pretty colours. Together we decided on a cream muslin frock that was just right for the occasion (and which she had probably been planning to wear all along, come to think of it). I helped her wash and change, then unpacked the cases and hung up the rest of her beautiful clothes while she wandered about the room, asking me a stream of questions about Swallowcliffe and the Vyes. She had already been so kind to me, taking the trouble to put me at my ease like that, and I'd have done anything for her in return. At least I was able to pass on what I knew about the Hall.

'I don't think I've ever seen such a beautiful place,' she said, wandering over to the window and looking out over the parkland and the hills behind. 'I mean to explore every inch of it, if I may. Don't bother about my hair, Polly – I cannot bear to sit still for a moment. Do you think I am sufficiently presentable to go downstairs?'

So that was Miss Brookfield. Everyone she came across ended up a little in love with her – man, woman and child – and I think we were all hoping that she in turn might fall in love with Master Edward. Quite apart from her being so wealthy (the only child of a shipping magnate, apparently), she would make a wonderful mistress for Swallowcliffe; she seemed to think as much of the house and grounds as we all did.

'They could live in one of the spare houses on the estate for the time being,' Mary said. 'Why, the Dower House is empty at the moment! That would be perfect. And her father would probably buy them a place in London for the season.'

We had everything worked out by the end of Miss Brookfield's first evening at the Hall: all that remained was for Master Edward to propose before she disappeared back to America, and for her to accept.

'Do you think she likes him?' I asked William, happening to come across him laying the breakfast room table the next morning. 'How did they get on last night?'

'They were talking about books for nearly half an hour,' he reported, 'and every one Master Edward mentioned, she'd read too. So that's a good sign. But Master Rory was sitting on her other side, and she seemed pretty taken with him. They're to go out riding tomorrow.'

Unfortunately Mr Wilkins was coming, or I would have spoken my mind about Master Rory. Trust him to stick his oar in and go spoiling things! Why didn't he leave Miss Brookfield alone and give his brother a chance? She would be just right for Master Edward – cheer him up a bit – and she would be just right for Swallowcliffe, too. Surely she would not turn down the chance of becoming the next Lady Vye, and everything that went with it?

The whole family showed Miss Brookfield and her mother around the estate. They were particularly taken with the boathouse, which apparently reminded them of the mountain chalets they had seen in Switzerland. Between them, Miss Brookfield, Edward and Rory came up with the idea of holding a surprise party for Miss Harriet's birthday there. Her brothers would take Harriet out rowing on the lake in the morning, and stop off at the boathouse as if by chance. Inside, all the guests would be waiting to wish her a happy birthday, with a wonderful luncheon spread out on the table.

'I know you will arrange everything perfectly,' Master Rory said to us in the servants' hall – no doubt hoping to win us over, since making the boathouse ready and then serving a meal there would be quite a performance. 'Let's give Harriet a party she'll remember!'

We all agreed that we would – although as Becky said afterwards, when Rory had left, she did not believe half so much fuss would have been made of Miss Harriet's birthday if Miss Brookfield had not been there to witness it. I couldn't get over Master Rory, standing there in front of Iris and talking about the boathouse, bold as brass. He might have spared a thought for her feelings. They had met there secretly at least once, to my knowledge, and maybe at other times too; surely he would have been able to persuade Miss Brookfield that the party might be better held somewhere else. I could tell that Iris was upset by it. She was sitting beside me and I felt her flinch when he mentioned the place.

Iris had taken a turn for the worse since Rory had returned to Swallowcliffe; all the spirit seemed to have gone out of her and I noticed her red-eyed a couple of times in the morning, as if she had been crying at night. I should like to box his ears for the trouble he's caused, I thought to myself as I swept out the grate in the boathouse, the day before Miss Harriet's birthday. There he was, parading about with Miss Brookfield as though he hadn't a care in the world, and breaking poor Iris's heart in the process.

'Well, I've done my best with the carpets but they still smell properly musty,' Jane said, coming in through the open double doors. 'And how everybody is to fit in here with all those tables and chairs, not to mention the food and drink and enough people to serve it, I really don't know.'

It had to be said, she could be a right misery sometimes. 'Oh, they'll manage,' I told her. 'It's sure to be sunny so most of them will sit out on the balcony, I should imagine.'

Despite my reservations about the boathouse from Iris's point of view, there was no denying it made a wonderful place to hold a party. It was so private and set apart, with the sparkling lake in front and a tangle of woods behind. That evening the gardeners brought in all sorts of potted plants and buckets full of pink roses; the place ended up so crammed with greenery and flowers you could scarcely make out an inch of bare wall. Edward, Rory and Miss Brookfield and her mother came to inspect the decorations while Jane and I were setting out the tables. The older lady was on the pernickety side, unfortunately, and wanted to rearrange everything to suit her own odd ideas, but Miss Brookfield was delighted. 'How pretty it looks,' she said, gazing around. 'Just like a room made out of leaves and branches. Harriet will love it!'

'What she will love most about her birthday is the fact that you are there to share it,' said Master Rory, looking at her all moony-eyed. 'I declare, Miss Brookfield, you have not even been at Swallowcliffe a week and already I cannot imagine the place without you. We shall be quite desolate when you are off on your travels again.'

'Then perhaps I can come back to cheer you up,' she said, with a pretty smile. 'If you will be kind enough to invite me, that is.'

'Good friends don't need an invitation,' said Master Edward, breaking in on the conversation. 'Whenever you'd like to visit, Miss Brookfield, we shall be delighted to see you.'

That's a bit more like it, I thought to myself, polishing a teaspoon on the corner of my apron.

I was glad to see that it was Edward who sang a duet with Miss Brookfield that evening while Miss Eugenie played the piano; he had a lovely rich voice. They were all late to bed, which made me late too, since I had to help Miss Brookfield out of her evening gown. It was a hot, close night, with faint rumblings of thunder in the distance and scarcely a breath of air in our room. I drifted uneasily in and out of sleep, and at one point found myself looking over towards Iris's bed. It was empty, just like before. I could not bear it; we weren't starting all this business up again, were we? I sat up and looked out of the window in case I should happen to find her by the lake again, although surely she would not have gone to the boathouse tonight. At any rate, the sliver of a new moon did not shed enough light for me to see.

Then, suddenly, I knew exactly where Iris would be. So it turned out: as I climbed through the sash window on to the roof, I saw her standing with her back to me, leaning against one of the chimney stacks and gazing out into the dark velvety sky. The hem of her nightgown fluttered a little in the faint breeze, but otherwise she was completely still. Something in the slope of her shoulders made me feel sadder than words could say, and when she turned her head, I saw that her cheeks were wet with tears.

'Oh, Iris,' I said, putting my arms around her, 'won't you tell me what is the matter? Could I not help you in some way?'

She shook her head, clinging to me for a moment. 'There is nothing anyone can do. Don't worry, I am sure it will turn out all right in the end.' She laid her head on my shoulder and I rubbed her back, feeling it was all I could do to comfort her.

We stood there like that for some minutes. 'You have been a good friend to me, dear Polly,' she said eventually. 'We have shared some happy times together, haven't we?'

'And many more to come, God willing,' I said, not wanting to follow where her words were leading me, and fighting against the hopeless tone of her voice. 'Now come inside or we shall never be up in the morning.'

The roof seemed a dangerous place for Iris to be in that state of mind, and I was relieved when she allowed me to lead her down and back into bed. I kissed her cheek and she closed her eyes, though I don't think either of us managed much sleep the rest of that long night.

TEN

Should you be required to walk with a lady or gentleman, in order to carry a parcel, or otherwise, always keep a few paces behind.

Do not smile at droll stories told in your presence, or seem in any way to notice, or enter into, the family conversation, or the talk at table, or with visitors; and do not offer any information unless asked, and then you must give it in as few words as possible. But if it is quite necessary to give some information unasked at table or before visitors, give it quietly to your master or mistress.

From *A Few Rules for the Manners of Servants in Good Families*, 1901

The next day dawned bright and hopeful. I laid a bunch of meadowsweet and dog roses on Miss Harriet's early-morning tray, together with a lavender bag that I had made for her birthday out of a scrap of lace. It was not much, but

I had embroidered it with her initials as well as I could, and she seemed very pleased.

'It's lovely, Polly. Look at your tiny little stitches! How can you possibly make them so neat? Oh, this is going to be the best birthday ever. It is such a lovely day, and I am to go out riding with Miss Brookfield after breakfast, and then boating with Rory and Edward.'

Miss Brookfield had instructions to keep Harriet well out of the way while we carried all the china and food out to the boathouse. Mrs Bragg had prepared her favourite dishes: game pie, salmon mayonnaise, lobster salad and a huge side of roast beef with a chunk of fresh horseradish to grate. There were strawberries and peaches from the greenhouse too, and Mrs Henderson had baked a walnut cake which Iris had iced and decorated most beautifully with crystallised violets and rose petals. I did not get a chance to speak to Iris privately that morning, but at least she seemed a little calmer at breakfast.

At one o'clock sharp the guests were all waiting in the boathouse, its gingham curtains drawn so as not to give away the surprise. I winked at Master John across the room; he was almost bursting with excitement, hopping up and down while the nurserymaid held his hand and tried to keep him quiet. We maids had been given permission to stand at the back and wish Miss Harriet a happy birthday; Miss Brookfield thought it would be a nice way to thank us for everything we had done. Everyone fell silent as we heard Harriet's voice come floating across the water, followed by the clunk of the boat's wooden hull against the jetty. Then, suddenly, I noticed that Iris was missing. She should have been there, especially as she had taken such trouble icing the birthday cake, and I knew that she had been looking forward to seeing the boathouse in all its glory.

Rory opened the door and Harriet came in, and there was a great deal of 'Oh, my goodness!', 'Look who's here!' and 'Are you sure you didn't realise?' but I could not enjoy any of it. I knew in my bones something was badly wrong. Slipping away from the party as soon as possible, I ran back along the path around the lake, then straight up the servants' staircase to our bedroom.

Everything of Iris's had gone. Her chest of drawers was empty, her coat no longer hung on the back of the door, and her bed had been stripped of its sheets. It was as though she had never existed.

I turned around instantly and ran downstairs, my heart pounding in my chest and my shoes clattering on the wooden floorboards. For once, I did not care whether Mrs Henderson or anyone else could hear me making more noise than was necessary. I rushed along the corridor and knocked on the door of her room.

'Please, ma'am,' I said quickly, upon being admitted, 'has something happened to Iris?'

Mrs Henderson laid down her pen and looked at me for a long moment. 'Miss Baker is no longer a part of this household,' she said. 'You are to forget all about her. I shall tell the rest of the household at supper. If I hear anyone so much as mention her name again, they will be dismissed. She has been a naughty, wicked girl and if you have any sense, you will learn a lesson from what has happened to her. Is that understood?'

'Yes, ma'am,' I said, and quietly let myself out.

The news was more of a shock to me than a surprise. There was no need to ask why Iris had been made to leave. I had had my suspicions for a while now, and when I had held her close the night before in her thin cotton nightgown, they were confirmed. Iris had got herself into trouble, of the worst kind: she was expecting a baby.

Of course we *did* talk about Iris between ourselves that night. We could not pretend that nothing had happened.

'I always thought she was no better than she should be,' Jane said. 'Well, now the pigeons have come home to roost! I wouldn't be in her shoes for anything.'

'Do you know who the father is?' Becky asked me. 'You and Iris were always going about together. Didn't she ever tell you?'

'No, she never did,' I replied, which was true enough. I did not want to mention Rory Vye's name and hear what they would have to say about that. 'And even if she had, I'd have kept it to myself. We've no business speaking badly of Iris behind her back. What has she ever been to all of us but a good friend? You were happy enough to have her running up and down the stairs with cups of beef tea, Jane, when you were poorly over Easter. There was no mention of her being so very wicked then, as I recall.'

They harumphed a bit at that, saying of course they were sorry about what had happened and they hadn't meant any harm, and we went to bed very sniffy with each other. Well, let them look sideways and whisper under their breath – I didn't care! I would never forget everything Iris had done for me: the good advice she had always been ready to give, the hundred and one little kindnesses that had made my life so much easier since the first day I had come to Swallowcliffe. She might have made a mistake, but show me the person who's never done that. And she was certainly paying a heavy price for it now. How frightened and alone she must be feeling! The sight of her empty bed made me sick with worry. There was a thunderstorm that night which cleared the muggy air; I lay there, listening to the rain drumming down on our roof, and prayed that she had found somewhere safe and dry to sleep.

The next day, life carried on just the same. A stone might have been thrown into our little pool, but the ripples had faded quickly away and now the water was smooth again – on the surface at least. A new maid moved into the still room within a matter of hours: Lucy, the head kitchenmaid. She was interviewed by Mrs Henderson in the morning and took over her new post that afternoon as Mrs Bragg had no objection. I had no choice but to get on with things, like it or not. The house guests were staying for another few days, so there were bedrooms to be cleaned and beds to be made, linen and towels to be changed, endless cans of hot water to be carried up and down stairs. There would be croquet on the lawn, tennis matches, picnics in the woods, and trips to the seaside to entertain our visitors.

Keeping the house running smoothly, that was all that mattered. I wondered whether anyone in the family knew that Iris had gone, and what they would have thought about it if they did. Would Master Rory even notice, or was he too taken up with Miss Brookfield to care? I should have liked to give him a piece of my mind – not that it would have done much good, of course, and I did not dare risk being dismissed myself. You might be thinking that it wasn't very loyal to Iris, going on with my work just the same, but what choice did I have? It was too late to change what had happened, and there was no sense in two of us being out on the streets.

I thought about Iris all the time, though. I should have

liked to talk about her with somebody kind and trust-
worthy; William, perhaps; but we did not often have a
chance to speak now that there were no fires to be laid, and
Iris's condition was a rather delicate topic to bring up with a
young man anyway – especially one who had been attached
to her. Miss Harriet was far too taken up with the visitors to
think about anything else and I could not properly discuss
things with her, either. She had lived a very sheltered life and
besides, Master Rory was her brother; it was all a good deal
too close to home. And then in the afternoon, I came across
Miss Harriet hurrying along the passage.

'Can I come and hide in your sitting room, Polly?' she
said breathlessly. 'I am trying to give Miss Habershon the
slip and she'll never come looking for me there.'

Being so worried and preoccupied, I answered her very
bluntly, I'm afraid. 'And why should Miss Habershon
waste her time searching for you? It would not kill you to
sit in the schoolroom for an hour or so. I should like
nothing better, myself.'

'That is a very sharp remark,' she said, looking at me
warily. 'Why are you so scratchy all of a sudden? Are you
tired?'

'Sorry, Miss Harriet.' I came to my senses a little too
late. 'I didn't mean to be rude.'

'I don't mind,' she said, 'but tell me what you are
thinking, and why you should be so cross.'

I decided to be honest, and hang the consequences. 'Well, not cross, exactly. But you see, I had to leave school when I was ten and a sad day for me, that was. I like Miss Habershon, she has been lending me books and we talk about all sorts of things. I think you are not treating her at all fairly and it's not like you. Just think of everything you have done for me!'

'You're my friend, though. We help each other, we are on the same side. Miss Habershon is so strict and severe! If you could see her glaring at me over a German grammar book you would not like her so very much, I assure you.'

'Perhaps she only wants you to make an effort.' The governess had never said as much, but I could imagine that she was at her wits' end with Harriet. I had seen the pair of them once in the schoolroom, Harriet staring out of the window with her arms folded and Miss Habershon looking fit to burst with impatience.

'Well, I shan't give her the satisfaction,' Harriet declared. 'The sooner she leaves the better.'

I could have taken her by the shoulders and given her a good shake! 'Better for you, perhaps, but maybe not for her,' I said, Iris not far from my mind. 'Have you ever asked yourself where she will go? And how do you think she'll feel, having to leave because she could not manage to teach you anything? Lady Vye won't give her a good character reference and who knows where she could end up. Miss Habershon might be full of learning and getting on for a lady, but she is still a servant like the rest of us. She and I are on the same side in that respect.'

I could see I'd got to Miss Harriet now. 'In that case I had better choose another hiding place,' she said stiffly. 'Goodbye, Polly. I am sorry we have to disagree.' And she turned on her heel and marched off down the corridor.

I felt dreadful, watching her go, but it was too late to take back what I had said. My words hung like a black cloud between us, and I might never have had a chance to clear the air. I shudder to think how things could have turned out.

Piecing together the afternoon's events from what I saw with my own eyes and what I learned afterwards, this is the gist of what happened. Miss Harriet did not manage to avoid her lessons for very long; wherever she went, Miss Habershon must have found her, because they ended up in the schoolroom together half an hour or so later. Then, after a little while, Mr Goddard brought a message for Miss Habershon from Lord Vye, asking for her help right away in translating a letter he had received from a German gentleman who bred gun-dogs (His Lordship being interested in buying a pair). Not wanting to lose Harriet again, Miss Habershon took the schoolroom key and locked the door from the outside so that she could not run off – not a good idea, looking back, but I suppose it seemed sensible at the time.

This is where I came into the picture, having been sent up to the schoolroom by Mrs Henderson to ask Miss Habershon whether she would be dining with the family or the children that night. I was just rattling the door and wondering why on earth it should be locked when Miss Habershon came hurrying back from Lord Vye's study with the key. She opened it and we went into the room together – to find it empty. There was no sign of Harriet anywhere, but the sash window had been pushed up, and a breeze ruffled the pages of an open book on her desk.

'Dear Lord!' Miss Habershon gasped, turning pale. 'Whatever has she done?'

We both ran over to the window and looked out, dreading what we might see. Harriet was about four or five feet below us, clinging precariously to the branches of an old wisteria which snaked its way up the side of the house. The climber was not strong enough to bear her weight and we could see it slowly tearing away from the wall, inch by inch. I could not move or think for the horror of it.

'Try to hold on!' Miss Habershon cried, hanging out of the window and reaching down her arm to see if she could touch Harriet. 'Oh, this is hopeless. Polly, you may be able to reach her. I will run downstairs.' And she was off like the wind.

I threw myself over the windowsill. 'Look up, Miss!' I said, leaning down as far as I possibly could without falling myself. 'Try to grasp my hand.' I was a good deal taller than Miss Habershon, and my fingers were not so very far above Harriet's head: if she stretched out her arm, she could probably touch them.

'I daren't move or I shall fall!' Harriet called shakily back. There was the most dreadful rending sound even as she spoke, and a whole section of the climber she was holding came away from the wall. We both screamed and she swayed sickeningly in front of my eyes, before managing to grab hold of a nearer branch to steady herself.

'Polly, I'm so frightened,' she whispered, and who could blame her. 'Help me!'

It was terrible, being so close and yet not able to do anything. 'It's all right,' I said, trying to sound confident. 'Try to take my hand when you're ready.'

'If I let go, I shall fall,' she said again, risking a quick look upwards.

'Just try,' I urged her. 'One step at a time.'

Very slowly, Harriet took one hand away from the branch. Then, suddenly, her foot slipped. She panicked and lost her balance, so that for a terrible second she was hanging from the wall by one arm alone, her legs thrashing about in the air. My stomach turned over, but somehow she managed to find a new foothold among the creaking, cracking

140

wisteria branches. Leaves and twigs fell in a shower on to the grass below; it looked a very long way down to me.

'I cannot do it,' she sobbed, laying her cheek against the wall.

'Yes, you can,' I said. 'Don't give up!'

Closing her eyes and flattening herself against the wall, she slowly took away her right hand and reached up again to find mine. The tips of our fingers touched, while the climber splintered and snapped around her. 'Nearly,' I said, stretching down as far as I possibly could. 'Just a little further now!'

We were in desperate trouble. Even if Harriet managed to grasp both my hands with her own, I was probably not strong enough to pull her back up through the window. How long could I hold on to her before she lost her grip and fell? Maybe long enough for help to arrive, that was our only hope. Her hand grazed mine again – and then, suddenly, there was no hope left. With a wrenching groan, the main trunk of the creeper finally tore away from the wall. Harriet made one last desperate lunge for my hand but already she was falling back into thin air, screaming and falling away from my outstretched arms, falling down and down to the ground.

Things would have been a lot worse if Miss Habershon hadn't been standing there below, that's for sure. It was impossible for her to catch Harriet from that height, but at least she managed to position herself underneath so that she could break her fall, and they both tumbled over together with a sickening thud. I could not tell from above whether either of them was dead or alive. By the time I had run downstairs and outside, however, Harriet was already sitting up.

'Oh, Miss! Are you all right?' I said, sinking to my knees beside her. 'Thank heavens! What on earth possessed you to do such a thing?'

Harriet would not answer: she was staring at Miss Habershon, who lay there on the grass without moving. 'I have killed her!' she whispered, her face as white as chalk. 'She is dead and it is all my fault.'

Thankfully, it turned out that Miss Habershon was not dead, only knocked unconscious for a few seconds. She was the more badly injured of the two, however. It turned out she probably had a couple of cracked ribs and certainly a broken wrist, while Miss Harriet escaped with bruises and a sprained ankle. Still, the whole thing could have been a great deal worse, and the three of us knew it. Nobody else ever found out what really happened; we decided to say that Harriet had been injured while learning to ride Miss Habershon's bicycle. She didn't know how to stop, so Miss Habershon had bravely stepped in her path. That was the story, and we kept to it. If anyone thought it strange that I should have wheeled the bicycle back to its home in the stables before fetching help, they did not say so – nor stop to wonder why there should have been not so much as a scratch on the contraption. Harriet told her stepmother the accident was her fault if it was anybody's, so Miss Habershon was thanked very kindly for her efforts and allowed as much time off to recover as she needed.

Miss Harriet and I had made up with each other quickly enough after our little falling out: I said sorry to her and she said sorry to me, and that only left one person out of the triangle.

'All right, I'll apologise to Miss Habershon,' Harriet said, 'but will you come with me, Polly? I don't want to go on my own.'

'She won't eat you,' I said, though I was happy enough to hold her hand – and curious to see how things would turn out, too.

Miss Habershon was sitting by the window with her wrist in plaster. There was no need for Harriet to have worried about seeing her: as soon as we came in, she started right off saying how unwise she was to have locked the schoolroom door, she should never have done such a foolish thing and she hoped that Harriet wouldn't hold it against her. Harriet could hardly get a word in edgeways! But then *she* said that Miss Habershon hadn't been so wrong, in her opinion, because she would have run away if she'd had the chance, and locking the door wasn't half so foolish as climbing out of the window. We laughed about that, and the long and the short of it was, Miss Habershon and Miss Harriet ended up quite friendly. Harriet said she would try harder at her lessons, and Miss Habershon said she would try to find something more interesting to teach her; she'd think up some way of squaring it with Lady Vye. So the accident brought some good with it, alongside the bad.

Well, now Miss Harriet was going to have to manage her life without me for a little while, because shortly after the house party was over I would be going home for my week's summer holiday. I had been putting money aside for the train fare and was hoping for a tip from Miss Brookfield to make up the shortfall; she was very generous, which is not something you find as a matter of course with wealthy people in my experience. To be honest, I could not wait to get away. Swallowcliffe seemed a different place without Iris, and life was particularly flat and dull after our guests and the Vyes went back to London at the end of July to catch the last of the season. Then they would be going straight up to Scotland from there in the middle of August for the grouse shooting (no one worth their salt would be left in the city by then). This time William went with them, since Thomas had taken a tumble down the cellar steps in the dark and got a black eye for his trouble.

I was sorry to see William go – and Miss Brookfield too, as we had become quite attached to each other. She did not seem to think that being a servant, I was not worth talking to, and had told me all sorts of interesting things about America: how vast it was, with mile upon mile of wild open country in the West, and what terrible things the settlers had had to put up with as they tried to carve out a life for themselves. (That wouldn't have been my cup of tea! I could hardly imagine anything worse.) But it was probably not goodbye for ever, since she had been invited back to Swallowcliffe in October for the first of the shooting parties.

'And Harriet has made me promise to go hunting with her,' she said. 'So I shall be turning up again, like the proverbial bad penny.'

'I'm very glad to hear it, Miss,' I said, quite truthfully. Rory was right: the house seemed to come alive when Miss Brookfield was in it. She was far too good for him, but Edward would be lucky to have her as a wife. If he had any sense, he would not let her slip away.

So all in all, my week's holiday was particularly welcome. Yet as I sat on the train, I could not help remembering when Iris and I had taken that same journey together back in the spring, and how happy we had been in each other's company. Where was she now, and how was she feeling? I hoped to goodness her parents had been prepared to take her back home: those Baptists can be a strict and unforgiving lot. The thought that she might be ill and miserable somewhere, all alone, was unbearable to me.

ELEVEN

As with the Commander of an Army, or the leader of any enterprise, so it is with the mistress of a house. Her spirit will be seen through the whole establishment; and just in proportion as she performs her duties intelligently and thoroughly, so will her domestics follow in her path.

From *Mrs Beeton's Book of Household Management*, 1861

'Don't you go worrying yourself to death about that Iris,' my mother said as we waited for the train that would take me back to Edenvale at the end of my holiday. 'She has made her bed and now she must lie on it. There's nothing you could do for the poor girl – her troubles are her own and she has to bear them herself. Whatever is the point in making yourself miserable too?'

'I should just like to know she is safe and well,' I said, looking down the railway track and hoping the train would not take long to arrive. It had been lovely at home but now

I wanted to be back at Swallowcliffe, with a bed to myself and room to breathe – which probably sounds very ungrateful and selfish, but that's the truth of it. A week had been long enough to remind me how stifling life could be in the village, with everyone so involved in each other's business and eager to pass judgement. Even my mother had disappointed me a little, I have to confess. I had not been sure whether to tell her about Iris, but she asked after my friend most particularly and so out the story had to come.

'Well, she's not the first to be led astray and I dare say she won't be the last,' my mother said at the end of it. 'I would have thought she'd have had more sense, mind. Just be sure you never make the same mistake, Polly my girl! Can you imagine how people round here would talk? I should never get over the shame of it.'

Her reaction seemed rather heartless to me, and I was sad that she could not find it in herself to be any more charitable. Had she forgotten how easily Iris had become a part of our family on Mothering Sunday? How sweet she had been with Martha and Tom, and how patiently she had listened to Lizzie? People were remarkably quick to wash their hands of her, in my opinion, and it hurt me that my mother should be the same. We talked no more about the matter that evening, keeping instead to safer subjects such as the new vicar, Reverend Chadwick, who was causing quite a stir in the village.

'You should hear his sermons!' my mother said, chuckling. 'He does get himself worked up about all sorts of odd things. But he sat up two nights in a row with poor Mrs Hammer when her time came, and he would give you the shirt off his back. He let Tom Ford have his very own shoes when the scoundrel said he had none to come to church in and that was why he stayed at home on Sundays. Goodness knows what Mrs Chadwick had to say about that! They have been married ten years, I gather, but they haven't been blessed with children which is a shame – Mrs Chadwick takes the Sunday School class and she's right motherly.'

I met the vicar's wife a few days later, when I went to visit Mrs Grimshaw next door who was laid up with arthritis. Mrs Chadwick had brought round some rosehip syrup for the old lady, and I could see at once what my mother meant. Such a kind, gentle face she had: rather round and plain, but the goodness shone out of it like a ray of warm sunshine. She knew our family quite well already, and I was glad to think my mother had someone she could call upon for help should it be needed.

What with visits to the neighbours, and playing with my sisters and brother, and sleeping in until nine or ten o'clock of a morning, my holiday passed happily enough. Yet it made me realise that Swallowcliffe was my home. I was a visitor in my mother's house – a welcome one, to be

149

sure, but now that Lizzie was growing so fast, there was hardly room to swing a cat in the cottage with me there too. I was ready to go back to work, and not as downcast on the journey home as one might have thought.

I found on my return that Harriet and Miss Habershon were getting on like a house afire. They spent their mornings in the schoolroom with Master John but I would often see them in the afternoon, rambling about the estate with specimens they had picked up: odd plants and jars of muddy water from the lake with things swimming about in it. I had a terrible shock one morning when I was cleaning Miss Harriet's room. There was a cloth spread over her table and underneath it lay the body of a hare, one eye taken out and the skin pinned back to expose the flesh and guts underneath. I have skinned plenty of rabbits for the cooking pot and thought nothing of it, but this unfortunate creature looked as though it had been tortured in some gruesome ritual. I put the cloth back pretty quick, I can tell you, and hung my head out of the window for a breath of fresh air.

'Whatever are you doing to that poor animal?' I asked Miss Harriet that evening when I brought in her hot water for washing.

'Studying its anatomy,' she replied. 'Don't worry, it was dead anyway – one of the dogs had caught it. We are only putting the body to good use.'

150

'If you say so, Miss.' It didn't seem such a very good use to me. 'Well, perhaps you could keep the nasty-looking thing in the schoolroom. I should think it will give you nightmares.'

'But John doesn't like to see it,' she said. (And who could blame the boy!) Then before I could say any more, she quickly changed the subject. 'Polly, you were quite right: there is nothing Miss Habershon doesn't know. Even mathematics and science. I cannot tell you how much more interesting those subjects are than French verbs – and to think I might never have found out if I hadn't tried to climb down the wall.'

Of course I was glad to see Harriet so happily occupied, but as the days went by I began to miss her friendship. She was too busy with books and experiments and such things to spend much time chatting or going for walks. I felt as though she were leaving me behind – silly, I know, since her life was always bound to take a different path from mine. But I couldn't help becoming rather downhearted, which was not like me at all. Up one minute and down the next; I could not help wondering when my life would get back on an even keel. In the park, the leaves on the horse chestnut trees turned to gold, and blackberries were ripening on the briars which clutched at my skirt as I walked alone in the woods. The swallows knew that summer was over: they had already left the reed beds to start their long journey south. Autumn was coming, with the frosty breath of winter close on its heels. Soon I would be shivering up in the attic and out on the front step at dawn while the wind whipped around my ankles; my feet would be swollen with chilblains, my fingernails black with coal dust and my hands cracked and sore.

Oh, I was in a sad and sorry mood, all right. And then, one day, I looked out of an upstairs window to see the afternoon sun slanting across the park, and the deer grazing quietly under the trees, and managed to remember how lucky I was. To live and work in such a place! I had no business complaining about a speck of cold. From the moment I decided to take myself in hand, everything seemed to become easier. One glorious day, Mrs Henderson told us that Jemima had found a new position as parlourmaid to a family in London and so would not be coming back to Swallowcliffe, which I must confess was very welcome news to me. A new maid came to replace her, and since she was nearer my age, we made a pair together (Jane moving up to work with Becky). She was a Welsh girl called Megan, with a smooth freckled face like a brown hen's egg and a sing-song voice that was hard to understand at first. Being a practical, happy sort of soul, she was just the tonic I needed. We also needed the extra pair of hands: the family were shortly due back from Scotland, and the first shooting party was to be held at the beginning of October.

Miss Brookfield was still in England so she had been invited, I was pleased to hear, along with various other smart guests – although not the Prince of Wales (despite Jemima's prediction), which was a relief to Mrs Bragg but a great disappointment to the rest of us.

'Did you miss me?' William teased, the first time we met again over the coal scuttle. I would not give him the satisfaction of knowing how much. It worried me that I had found myself thinking about him when he wasn't there and counting the days until he came back. And yet before long he would probably be moving on too: no doubt a job would come up that was better paid or more to his liking in some way, and I would lose another friend. It was safer not to become too attached to anyone, I decided – and especially not to a person like William, who was kind and helpful to everyone and didn't mean anything by it. Megan was very taken with him after he'd carried her trunk upstairs, but I don't think he did that because he liked her in particular. At least I hoped not. But there again, he was free to like whomever he wanted; it had nothing to do with me.

A couple of days later, we heard news of another departure that came as a great shock to me. 'The new governess is to leave at the end of the month,' Mary told us at teatime. 'Shame, I thought this one would have lasted a little longer – she has not even been here a year. And Miss

Harriet seems to like her well enough, which makes a change.'

I had talked to Miss Habershon only days before about her plan to take Miss Harriet to visit the museum in South Kensington; she had not mentioned anything being wrong then. Just when things were going so well for the two of them! It was as though Lady Vye were determined that Harriet should be unhappy for one reason or another. 'Why does Miss Habershon have to go?' I asked, but nobody had any idea.

'Because my stepmother came into the schoolroom yesterday and saw what we were studying,' Harriet told me that night, white with anger. 'She says chemistry is an unsuitable subject for a girl. First Nanny Roberts and now Miss Habershon. I hate her, Polly. I wish she were dead!'

'Don't you ever say such a dreadful thing.' Of course Harriet was upset, but that kind of remark did not help anyone. 'Maybe she will change her mind if you explain how you feel. Or maybe she will let Miss Habershon stay if you take up French and piano again. That would be better than nothing, wouldn't it?'

'You don't understand! I am going to be a doctor, so I *have* to carry on studying sciences.'

'You can't be a doctor, Miss,' I said, trying not to smile. Wherever had she got that extraordinary idea from? 'Leave that sort of thing to the gentlemen.'

'There is a medical college in London entirely for women,' Harriet said impatiently. 'Miss Habershon has told me all about it. I mean to go there when I am eighteen, and I shall, one way or another. It is the only thing I have ever truly wanted to do.'

'And you have said as much to Her Ladyship, I suppose?'

Harriet nodded. Well, that explained it: no wonder Lady Vye wanted Miss Habershon out of the door and quick about it, too. Fancy planting such a peculiar notion in Harriet's head! 'How could a young lady like you ever treat someone who was sick or injured?' I asked her. 'What if it was some great strapping fellow who had broken his leg, or caught some horrible disease like smallpox – or worse?' Really, it didn't bear thinking about.

'But I want to look after women,' Harriet told me, her eyes lit up. 'Women like my mother who die having babies, or die trying *not* to have them. There are such dreadful things going on, Polly! You should hear what Miss Habershon has to say about the back streets of London. Don't you think women in those sorts of difficulties might prefer to see a lady doctor?'

I could not think past the words 'lady doctor', they sounded so strange to my ears. Harriet had certainly surprised me: she knew more about the world than I would ever have imagined. Her next remark was even more astonishing. 'What about Iris, for instance?' she said.

'I know she was dismissed, and I have an idea why. You would like to think that somebody kind and gentle was there to help her, wouldn't you? Somebody who did not think she was a wicked creature who ought to be punished?'

Of course I would, though I could not bring myself to say so. I did not want to talk about Iris with Miss Harriet, somehow. It was hard to think past the fact that Harriet was a Vye; I felt as though, between them, the Vyes had chewed Iris up and then spat her out. They might very well have known who was the father of her baby, but they didn't care what happened to her or the child.

'Have you heard from Iris?' Miss Harriet asked me. 'I keep wondering how she is.'

I had been unfair to her and felt ashamed; Harriet was a better person than that. She had no more power to help Iris than I did, however, and unfortunately there was not much I could do to help her in this predicament either.

'Just hold your fire for a couple of days,' I said. 'You'll have a better chance of persuading Her Ladyship when the guests have gone and things have quietened down.'

TWELVE

Good mistresses take an interest in the welfare and well-being of their servants; and thus gain an influence over them for good; but this is a very different thing to encouraging them in idle gossip, as a servant once permitted to become a narrator too often draws the long bow, and fact is lost in fiction.

From *The Duties of Servants: A Practical Guide to the Routine of Domestic Service*, 1899

'Do you know, Polly, I really cannot bear the thought of another afternoon's shooting. Would it be considered very bad form if I came back to the house straight after lunch?'

Miss Brookfield's lovely face appealed to me from the mirror while I put up her hair. (She had particularly asked for me as her maid again, which pleased me a great deal.) 'I'm sure no one would mind, Miss,' I said. 'You could always say you had to keep your mother company.'

'Anything would be better than hanging about in the

cold, staring up at the sky with that dreadful noise dinning on in one's head.' She sighed. 'How can Edward pretend to enjoy it so much?'

Things between herself and Master Edward seemed to be progressing very nicely, we were all glad to see. William told me that they had spent a lot of time together in London and then up in Scotland, visiting castles and walking over the moors. Master Rory had been called back to serve with his regiment by then which gave Edward a clear run at the field, so to speak, although Rory was back at Swallowcliffe for the shooting this weekend. The Brookfields were here again for a week before setting off for Italy; we maids were secretly hoping that Master Edward would propose to Miss Brookfield before they left. William had happened to notice that an envelope addressed to Miss Brookfield's father in America, in Edward's handwriting, had been left out for Mr Goddard to post. It was awkward that her family should be so far away. How long would a reply take to come?

I wondered whether Miss Brookfield knew about the letter. Of course I could not raise the matter with her, even though we had talked about all sorts of things together, so I bit my tongue and concentrated on her hair. 'There! I hope that will not come undone.'

She put a hand up to the back of her head to check. 'I

shouldn't think so. Lord, Polly, any more pins and I shall turn into a porcupine!'

'Do you want me to take some out? I was just thinking, what with the wind and everything—'

'No, you're quite right. I was only teasing. So, how do I look?'

'Perfect,' I said, and not a word of a lie. She was wearing a slim tweed skirt and fitted coat in the softest shade of heather, with a fox fur to throw around her shoulders – quite the English country lady.

She walked over to the fire and stood in front of it for a few minutes, warming her hands and gazing into the flames. 'Oh, don't listen to me grumble! It is so lovely to be back at Swallowcliffe again. If it wasn't for the fact that we shall be seeing Florence and Venice and Rome, I could hardly bear to leave. Still, at least we shall be coming back here for Christmas, so it is not to be goodbye for ever just yet.'

'I'm very glad to hear it.' Perhaps Master Edward would wait until then to ask for Miss Brookfield's hand. He had better not leave it too long, though, or somebody else would snap her up.

'I shall bring you back a souvenir – some Venetian glass, perhaps. Now, pass me my hat and I am ready for the fray. There, that will have to do. Until this afternoon, then, Polly!'

This was the pattern of a day's shooting at Swallowcliffe: the gentlemen and whichever ladies were interested (usually only Lady Vye and Mrs Trevelyan, a large widow who farmed near by) went off in the brake around ten o'clock for a couple of drives, to get their eye in. The rest of the ladies joined the party for an early luncheon somewhere in the woods at noon. It was never much of a meal, Lord Vye being keen to continue with the sport: just soup, bread and cheese for the beaters and gun loaders, and baked potatoes with Irish stew or some such for the ladies and gentlemen. Then off they went shooting again until the light began to fail, although most of the ladies would have trickled back to the house well before then and would be playing cards or writing letters by the fire.

It was a glorious day, that Saturday: bright and crisp, the sun shining down out of a clear blue sky and the ground thick with a rustling carpet of golden-brown leaves. Miss Brookfield and Master Rory came back together from the shooting after luncheon, and I helped my young lady change into a riding habit. She said the afternoon was far too good to waste sitting inside and they were going out for a gallop. I didn't like the sound of that at all. Master Rory appeared to the very best advantage, sitting on a horse; even I had to admit that he looked particularly dashing in the saddle. Miss Brookfield looked quite radiant, I noticed, which worried me too – as though she were lit up from inside by some secret glow of happiness. I had seen that look before: it had been on Iris's face as she went off to the ball. I hoped to goodness that Master Edward was the cause of it this time and not his brother.

'Goodbye, Miss,' I said. 'Be careful, won't you?'

'We shall keep out of the way of the guns,' she said, laughing – although that was not what I had meant at all.

I had no time to spare fretting about Miss Brookfield, however; with a houseful of guests there was plenty to be getting on with. We had all sorts of people staying at the Hall, from Lord Vye's older sister and her husband (the Duke and Duchess of Hamworthy) who had come for the shooting, to a very well-known lady gardener by the name of Miss Dorothy MacIntyre who had come to look at Lord Vye's hothouses. I had thought a gardener might be taking her meals with us in the servants' hall, but not a bit of it. Miss MacIntyre was given the Red Room, the finest guest bedroom in the whole house, and Mary told me the Vyes saw it as a great honour to have her to stay. She did not actually do much work in the garden, I gathered (although you might have thought so from the state of her clothes, which were decidedly shabby), but rather told people what they should be planting and where. The only trouble was, Lord Vye was too taken up with the shooting to pay Miss MacIntyre much attention, so Harriet and Miss Habershon ended up taking her round the hothouses and the gardens. It would have been better for her to have come another weekend, in my opinion, but she seemed to have hit it off with Miss Habershon and wasn't too put out not to have His Lordship as a guide.

I was tidying up in the Red Room whilst they were gone, wondering whether Miss MacIntyre had brought a gown that I should lay out for her to change into later (she didn't seem to have anything suitable, but surely she couldn't take tea in those moth-eaten old tweeds) when the idea suddenly struck me that a lady gardener might be a very good person for Miss Harriet to have on her side.

'Perhaps you could persuade her to drop a word in Her Ladyship's ear about your studies,' I said to Harriet, when she was changing for tea herself. (The children always went down to the drawing room to chat with the Vyes' guests for an hour or so at that time, to give them practice as to how to behave in company.) 'Why, she might even know about this medical college you were talking about – the type of lady she is. She could tell Lady Vye it was a respectable place.' If that was the case; I still had my doubts.

'Do you really think she would help me?'

'No harm in asking. Why don't you have a word with her about it now, before she goes downstairs?'

Miss Harriet thought about that for a while. 'Perhaps I shall. At least it's worth a try.'

*

It was getting dark by the time Miss Brookfield and Master Rory came back from their ride. Nobody else was about — tea was already being served in the drawing room — but I had been putting coats away in the downstairs cloakroom, and saw them walk in through the back door from the stables. They didn't notice me; they were far too wrapped up in each other. Rory had opened the door for Miss Brookfield. As she walked through, she looked up at him with such a weight of meaning in her eyes: shy and bold at the same time somehow, and questioning, as though she were waiting for him to speak. Neither of them said a word, however. They stood there, looking at each other in silence for a good few seconds, and then Rory lifted her hand to his lips and kissed it. I shrank back into the shadows with a heavy heart, wishing I hadn't had to see them.

Miss Brookfield rested in her room until dinner, and she was very thoughtful while I helped her change into a beautiful black brocade gown, with a bodice of black net embroidered all over in gold thread and little gold stars. How I wished I could have talked to her, as one friend to another! But of course we were maid and mistress, no matter how friendly she acted towards me, so it was out of the question. Well, it was shaping up to be quite an evening.

When I brought hot water to Miss Harriet's room a little

while later, she had two pieces of news to share. The first was that Miss MacIntyre had turned up trumps. She thought it was 'perfectly splendid' that Harriet should want to be a doctor, couldn't imagine a finer governess than Miss Habershon, and had promised to think of a way to bring Lady Vye round to the idea. The second was that Harriet had wormed out of her brother Edward the fact that he planned to ask Miss Brookfield to marry him before she went to Italy, and that he was probably going to propose this very night, after dinner.

'Surely she must say yes,' Megan sighed, as we discussed the matter while collecting our cleaning boxes from the housemaids' pantry after our own supper. 'She seems to like him well enough.'

'But you can't help thinking she'd have more fun with Master Rory,' Becky said. 'They are as alike as two peas in a pod! Master Edward is far too solemn for her.'

'She needs somebody like that to keep her feet on the ground,' Jane said. 'Besides, if she marries him she will be mistress of Swallowcliffe one day, and that must give her pause for thought.'

I couldn't bear to say anything, and only hoped with all my heart that Miss Brookfield would come to the right decision. Dinner came and went, and we were on tenter-hooks for any news. Apparently, she and Master Edward spent some time alone together out on the terrace (it being too cold for Mrs Brookfield to chaperone her daughter and everyone else having the sense to stay indoors), but there was no announcement made after they came back in, and nobody knew quite what had passed between them.

Miss Brookfield was still unusually quiet when she came up to her room for the night. 'Could you bring me a glass of warm milk, please?' she asked, after I had helped make her comfortable and was about to leave. 'Something tells me I shall have trouble sleeping.'

That was the only reference she made to anything being out of the ordinary – except that when I came back with the milk a little while later, she suddenly asked me, 'Have you ever found, Polly, that your heart tells you one thing and your head another? Which is the right one to follow, do you think?'

'Perhaps you should wait until they're both leading you in the same direction,' I said. 'Although I would trust my head over my heart if I had to choose between them.'

Miss Brookfield went off to Italy a couple of days later with the matter of Master Edward's proposal still hanging in the air. She hadn't said yes, Mr Goddard told Mr Wilkins who told Mary, who told Becky, Jane, Megan and me – but she hadn't said no, either. Edward would have to wait for her decision until Christmas, and so would the rest of us.

And what of the plan to save Miss Habershon? 'It

worked like clockwork,' Miss Harriet told me the next day. 'If only I could have been there to see what happened! Miss MacIntyre told my stepmother how impressed she was by my knowledge of plants, and how excellently I had been taught. Was there any chance she might be persuaded to part with that young governess, because she happened to know that the Gore-Smythes were in urgent need of a tutor for their three daughters and Lord Gore-Smythe hadn't been able to find anyone in London with the slightest knowledge of botany, let alone any of the other sciences. And he was prepared to pay up to forty guineas a year.'

'Wasn't that a risk?' I asked. 'What if Her Ladyship had said yes?'

'But she wouldn't, you see – that was the clever part. If Lord Gore-Smythe's daughters are to be taught science, then it must be the done thing and perfectly all right for me. The Gore-Smythes set the tone in London, Miss MacIntyre says – she has designed their garden in Eaton Square. Then, apparently, someone leaned across the table and said that if there was any talk of the Vyes' governess being let go, they would like to have her for *their* children and would pay quite as much as Lord Gore-Smythe if not more because she was obviously quite a find.'

More than forty guineas! Some folk certainly have more money than sense, I thought to myself.

'So then,' Harriet went on, 'my stepmother said very

firmly that Miss Habershon was staying at Swallowcliffe for the foreseeable future, and she hoped no one would think of trying to tempt her away. She asked to see Miss Habershon this morning, and told her that there seemed to have been some misunderstanding – she would like her to continue to teach me and would leave the subject matter in her hands, so long as I worked hard.'

'Well, good for Miss MacIntyre. Only, it might be a good idea not to mention this medical college for a while. No sense in pushing things, is there?'

'Maybe not,' Harriet admitted. 'I shan't forget about it, though.'

'I'm sure you won't,' I said, smiling as I went back to the grate.

So that was Miss Harriet settled, and one problem off my mind. The days passed, November arrived and one morning a new smell floated through the Hall: dark brown, sweet and spicy. Mrs Bragg was making mincemeat and plum puddings. Before we knew where we were, Christmas would be here. I found myself thinking about Iris a great deal of the time; she had probably had her baby by now, and I prayed for them both every night. And then one morning, almost as though I had willed it by wishing so hard, I opened my mother's weekly letter to find a note folded inside, and knew instantly that it had come from

Iris. She must have known her handwriting might have been recognised and the letter opened, had she sent it directly to the Hall.

'I have been in two minds for some time as to whether to pass this on,' my mother wrote, 'but seeing how anxious you were about your friend, I thought you should like to have word from her. Of course you cannot visit the workhouse (how could she ever suggest such a thing!) but at least you know she is alive and has been safely delivered.'

This is what Iris had written to me:

20 November 1890

My dearest Polly,
I hope this letter reaches you, and that your mother will forgive me for sending it to her in the first instance. How are you, my dear friend? I think of you often and wonder what is happening at Swallowcliffe. It seems a very long way from here, although in fact I am fewer than fifteen miles away. Please do not be too shocked when I tell you that I was admitted to the workhouse in Hardingbridge a little while ago. My parents did not want to take me back at home on account of the shame I have brought upon the family, which was much as I expected. But the workhouse is not such a bad place, and last week my baby was born here — a

beautiful boy – which may shock you too, although I think you must have known he was on the way. Do you think too badly of me? I hope not, because I have something very important to ask you.

Would you come and see me? We are not allowed visitors as a rule but I have said that you are my sister and so they have permitted me one visit. I know this may be difficult for you to arrange, but can you come in three weeks' time, on the morning of Sunday, 14 December? That is when they will allow me to see you. You can take the train to Hardingbridge, it is only a few stops further down the line from Little Rising. The workhouse is in Union Street – everyone knows where it is.

You may feel uncomfortable about being seen in such an establishment, which I quite understand, but there is really nothing to fear. Please come if you can, Polly dear – I must talk to you about an urgent matter. You may well not want to see me again, but could you find it in your heart to grant this request, for old times' sake? I have no one else to ask, and there is no other soul in the world I would rather see than you.

Do not desert me, I beg you,
Your loving friend,
Iris Baker

The workhouse! As soon as I read that word, the rest of the letter seemed to dissolve in front of my eyes. To think of my lovely, sweet Iris ending up in such a place! I had to read her note several times to take in the rest of it, and then another set of worries came thick and fast. My mother had shilly-shallied so long in sending on the letter that Sunday 14 December was a matter of days away. It would be near on impossible to arrange for time off to visit Iris at such short notice – and pay for the train fare, besides. We would not get our last quarter's wages until after Christmas, and I only had two shillings to my name.

I laid the letter aside with Iris's final words sounding in my head: 'Do not desert me, I beg you.'

How could I let her down?

THIRTEEN

The Workhouse should be a place of hardship, of coarse fare, of degradation and humility; it should be administered with strictness, with severity; it should be as repulsive as is consistent with humanity.

The Revd H. H. Milman, 1832

It was a long walk up Union Street to the workhouse, and not made any shorter by the crowd of noisy children who left off playing in the road to follow behind me, laughing and shouting. When I came to a stop outside the porter's lodge, the jeers rose to a crescendo and a stone came whizzing through the air very close to my head. By the time I turned around, they had already taken to their heels, so I vented my feelings on the door knocker instead and gave it a good hammering.

The door flew open and I found myself looking into the watery eyes of an elderly gentleman with flushed cheeks, a bulbous red-veined nose and two of the bushiest grey sideburns I had ever seen.

'All right, all right!' he said irritably. 'Why should you be in such a hurry to enter this place, young lady?'

'Sorry, sir,' I replied, 'my nerves are all in a jangle this morning.' There was no point in getting on the wrong side of him – you catch more flies with honey than with vinegar, as my mother likes to say.

'Aye, as well they might be,' he said, not unkindly. 'Most folks who come this way finds themselves all jangled up in one way or another. And they look a darn sight worse than yourself, in the main.'

'But I have only come on a visit, not to stay.' I hurried to put him right. 'My fr— my sister is here, and I am to see her today.'

'Oh, are you indeed? And have you brought your calling card? We likes things done proper here! I shall have to announce you in the droring room!' And he collapsed into a paroxysm of the most dreadful wheezing which I eventually realised was what passed for laughter. This soon turned into a proper coughing fit, so I patted the old fellow on the back and waited until he could speak again.

'I shall unlock the gate, Your Ladyship,' he gasped. 'Stay there.' And the door slammed shut again.

The porter's lodge was set at one side of a gated arch, through which I could see the grey bulk of the workhouse itself. It was a forbidding stone building, with row upon row of narrow windows frowning down onto a bleak courtyard below. I shivered, and not merely because it was a cold, damp day that seemed to have frozen the very marrow in my bones.

'The Archway of Tears, that's what folks calls it around here,' the porter said, shutting the gate behind me with a clang and locking it up again. 'You'll be glad enough to pass through the other way, I'll be bound, but spare a thought for the poor souls who never will. Now, come this way.'

He took me into his lodge through a door on the other side of the arch, then out by another door at the back into a passage which led along to a large, bare room. It was empty except for a table, the chair behind it and a bench opposite. 'Wait here for the matron,' he said. 'I've rung for her to collect you.' I took a seat on the bench and tried to think of cheerful things so as not to lose heart completely.

Matron appeared a short while later, and any cheerful thoughts vanished right away. She matched the building very well, having a face that might have been carved from the same stone. 'Unbutton your coat,' she said, by way of a greeting. 'If you've brought in any drink, it'll be the worse for you.' And she glared at me most severely while she searched for it, as though she could read on my face the thousand naughty intentions that were no doubt in my mind.

173

'Right, follow me,' she said when this unpleasant process was over, and marched briskly the other way down the corridor, which skirted the open courtyard. It was a little after midday, and we went past the open doorway of a dining hall filled with row upon row of women, all seated facing the same way and dressed in the same blue-and-white striped dresses, some with grubby calico shifts over them. The next room contained rows of men in striped cotton shirts. I wondered where the children were: they must have been in another part of the workhouse. Nobody spoke a word; the only sound to be heard was the scraping of spoons upon plates and an occasional shifting of benches. A thin, sour smell that might once have had something to do with boiled beef and turnips hung on the air.

We went on down the passage, past a large laundry room, round a corner and then up two flights of stairs. At last Matron stopped at a door halfway along the upper landing. 'This is where the unchaste women are. You can have half an hour with your sister and no more,' she rapped out to me. 'I will come back for you when the time is up.' She opened the door, and in I went.

Iris was sitting in a chair facing the door, wearing one of those same striped dresses. Her face lit up when she saw me. 'Polly! You came!' She made as if to get up, though it was too much for her and she sank back in the chair, staring at me as though she could not quite believe I was really there. Although she was clearly overjoyed to see me, I could tell she was also ashamed that I should have had to find her in such a place.

'Well, of course I did! Now don't you go disturbing yourself on my account. You stay there and I shall sit beside you.'

Settling her back in the chair gave me a moment to gather my wits, because I should not have liked Iris to see how shocked I was at the sight of her. Her beautiful golden hair had been hacked short – the way Mother cuts our Tom's when he's been especially naughty – and the pink and white softness of her skin had faded to a dirty grey. She looked exhausted and ill, and every so often her body shook with a hollow, racking cough. What worried me most, however, was the desperate look in her eye: as though she had already endured more than a body ever should, and knew her troubles were not yet over.

'You'll have to sit on the floor, then,' said a gravelly voice. 'Not exactly set up for visitors, are we?'

A heavy, blowsy-looking woman was staring at us both with great interest from her seat on a low bed in a corner of the room. She had dark, bedraggled hair which stood out in all directions like a moulting feather duster, and when she drew back her narrow lips to smile at me in welcome, I could see that most of her teeth had rotted away to blackened stumps. She might have been forty or even fifty, yet there was a wooden crate on the dusty floor beside the bed with a swaddled shape laid in it that must have been a baby.

'This is Miss Harker,' Iris told me, and I knew from her face that she could tell what I must be thinking.

'Pleased to make your acquaintance,' the lady said. 'Call me Lily. We don't stand on ceremony here, do we, Iris?' She smiled again. 'Iris and Lily – two lovely flowers in a field.' And she laughed, which was not a pleasant sound.

Then I noticed another wooden box on the floor, not far from where I was kneeling beside Iris's chair. She nodded proudly. 'There is my Ralph. Take a peek at him, Polly, if you'd like.'

Of course I would. I have always loved babies – their soft downy heads and the sweet milky smell of them – and I could not wait to see Iris's. Such a wise round face looked back at me from the depths of the blanket! He was wide awake but not making a sound, just gazing up at that cracked, cobwebby ceiling as though it was the bluest, most heavenly sky in the world.

'Oh, there's a dear,' I whispered, stroking his peachy cheek with my little finger. 'Iris, he's perfect!'

'You can pick him up if he's awake,' she said. 'He seems to like being cuddled.'

Lily tutted in exasperation. 'Why can't you leave him

alone for five minutes? I've told your sister a hundred times, she'll spoil the bairn, always petting and fussing over him.'

I ignored her and lifted up the little bundle to settle him against my shoulder. If only Iris and I could have been alone together! There was so much to say but we could hardly talk with that dreadful Lily there. I wished she would step outside to give us some privacy.

Iris watched me hungrily as I held her baby. 'Here, you have a turn,' I said, offering him over, but she shook her head.

'No, you keep him.' I could see she was very close to tears. Then she raised herself up a little in the chair, cleared her throat and said, 'Mrs Henderson gave you the day off? That's a wonder.'

I did not go into the full story behind my coming to the workhouse, not wanting to worry her. I had had to tell Mrs Henderson that my mother had suddenly been taken ill (which I hated to do, being superstitious about lying over such things) and plead with her to be allowed home for the whole day. She hummed and hahed about it, but at last she said yes, so then all I had to do was persuade someone to lend me the train fare – not an easy task with Christmas coming up. Luckily Megan came to my rescue, having some money put aside for a rainy day.

So Iris and I wasted time talking about this and that,

while the minutes of my visit ticked by and Ralph nuzzled against my shoulder. Now it seemed as though she could hardly bear to look at the baby, which was strange.

'Don't think *I* shall be carrying him around like that all day,' Lily said, watching me walking to and fro with obvious disapproval.

'Lily is to leave the workhouse next week and she has offered to keep Ralph for a while, until I can come for him,' Iris explained. 'I am sure it will not be for long, but I need to get a little stronger before leaving myself.'

I looked at her for a moment without speaking, trying to understand what she was telling me with her eyes. Something important, it had to be. Luckily, Lily's child set to wailing just at that moment – a thin, reedy cry that did not seem to hold out much hope of an answer. The noise went on, and Lily went on ignoring it. Then a bright idea came into my head: I laid Ralph back on the rough, straw-stuffed mattress in his cot and took out my purse.

'Your baby must need feeding, and I'm sure you won't want a stranger looking on. Perhaps you could take the mite downstairs for a moment? Here's a shilling for your trouble.' It was all the money I had left.

The sight of my purse made Lily a good deal more considerate, and she took herself off the bed in quite a hurry to test the coin with one of her few remaining teeth. 'Just for a few minutes, then,' she said, and yanked the baby up out of its box – which gave the poor thing such a shock that it stopped crying immediately.

As soon as they had gone, Iris started talking more freely. 'I don't want Lily to take Ralph, Polly. She's no fit person to look after a baby, anyone can see that. I have a little bit of money put aside, you see, for after he was born. I had to give it to the matron for safe keeping when I came in here, and now Lily knows about it too – she and the matron are thick as thieves. She says she will take care of Ralph if I pay her five shillings a week, and I can come for him when I'm feeling better.' Her words ended in a paroxysm of coughing, which she tried to stifle with a grubby handkerchief. 'They mean to take him away from me, I know they do, and what will become of him then? But I'm not strong enough to stand up to them.'

'Hush, hush,' I said, wiping the hair off her damp brow. 'Don't upset yourself.' Poor thing, she was burning up! I saw to my dismay that the handkerchief at her mouth was spotted red with blood, and had to look away so she would not see the tears in my eyes.

'Ralph is all that matters. Give him to me, Polly.'

I put the baby gently into her arms and she laid her hollow cheek against his soft round one. 'I cannot help loving him,' she whispered. 'They say all my wickedness has been passed on to him, but how can that be? He is an innocent child, sent from God.'

'And what of his father?' It was an awkward question, but I had to ask.

She smiled sadly. 'His father gave me the money to get rid of him. Not such a fine gentleman after all, as it turned out.' For a second she clutched the little scrap to herself as though she would never let him go, then tenderly she kissed the top of his head and passed him back to me. 'You take him,' she said. 'Please, Polly! This is no place for a baby, and I am too sick to care for him now.'

'Take him where? Whatever are you asking me to do?'

'Take him away from here! I thought your mother might agree to bring him up until he has grown into a lad, and perhaps he could be apprenticed in some trade—' She began coughing again and the handkerchief went up to her mouth. 'He will be such a fine young man,' she went on when she had recovered herself. 'Every night I dream about him living in your cottage, with your little brother Tom for a playmate. I know it is a lot to ask, but for the love of God, Polly, please help me!'

I had never in my life seen anyone so desperate. The baby had started fussing on my lap, so I gave him my finger to hold and looked down into his solemn blue eyes while I tried to decide what to do. He had a strong grip, that was for sure – as though he were determined to hang on to whatever chances came his way and not let go in a hurry.

'If you tuck him into your shawl and then button up your coat, no one will know he is there,' Iris went on. 'Hurry, please! Lily will be back in a minute – she does not trust me an inch. And don't let the matron see you, whatever happens. Go, now! Quickly, Polly, or you will meet her on the way out!'

What else could I do? Even though I knew my mother would never in a month of Sundays take Iris's baby, even though there was almost certainly no chance of us leaving the workhouse undiscovered, even though I would end up in terrible hot water, I laid Ralph against my chest and Iris dragged herself out of the chair to help me bind the shawl tightly around him. For a second we clung to each other with the baby sandwiched between us.

'Will you tell him about me?' she whispered. 'Tell my little boy he had a mother who loved him dearly, however weak and foolish she might have been.'

I nodded, not being able to speak at that moment. Then she took something out of the folds of her dress and pressed it into my hand. 'This is all I have to give him.' It was a tiny photograph of herself behind the still room table, smiling out at Master Edward's camera as though she hadn't a care in the world. 'Oh, but it will get crumpled and torn!' She fell back into the chair with her hands over her face. 'He will never know me. It is all for nothing.'

I knelt beside her, careful not to squash the baby.

181

'Remember my locket? I shall put your picture in there and give it to Ralph so he can look at it when he has grown into that fine young man and see what a lovely mother he has. He will not forget you, Iris, whatever happens – I will make sure of that. And neither shall I. God bless you.'

'Thank you,' she said, a hand still covering her eyes. 'Now, go. Run!'

I understood why she could not bring herself to look at Ralph for one last time. Her heart was breaking in front of my very eyes; if I did not take the baby now, she would lose the courage ever to let him go. So I left the room without another word.

I ran into trouble straight away. The sound of a heavy tread on the stairs and a dispirited wail alongside it told me that Lily was coming – and she was not far away. If I carried on down the passage, we would run straight into each other. Quickly, I turned the other way and tried the door of the next room along. It was not locked, thank the Lord; I slipped inside to hide for a moment, praying the place would be empty. The room was completely bare, with only the narrowest slit of a window set high up in the far wall. This wall, like the other three, was covered from top to bottom with some sort of heavy material, and a pair of leg irons was chained to the floor. I shuddered and hugged Ralph to me, as much for my comfort as his. We had fetched up in a padded cell, designed so the poor souls who ended up there would not be able to injure themselves or anyone else. Iris was right: the workhouse was no place for a baby.

When I could see through a crack in the door that Lily had reached the nursery and then gone back inside, I seized my chance and dashed back along the corridor as though all the hounds of Hell were after me. Down the first flight of stairs I flew, holding Ralph's head against my chest so he would not be jolted over-much, and then down the next, pausing only for a few seconds to listen out for the matron. It was dangerous to run, but I had no choice; there was not a moment to spare. 'Quietly now, Ralph,' I whispered as we hurried down the long corridor. I could see the inmates shuffling dejectedly around outside in the exercise yard, as though they had given up the will to live. I hoped the matron was safely tucked away in her warm office. Quickly, I sped along the final passage to the porter's lodge and rapped on his door. How long would he ever take to answer?

'First she's all in a rush to get in, now she can't wait to leave,' he grumbled, fumbling for an age to find his keys. 'So how did you enjoy the visit, Your Ladyship?'

'Quite well, thank you,' I said, fighting to control my ragged breathing as I listened out for the clamour behind me that was bound to follow.

'Not making off with any of our valuables, are you?' he

asked, giving me a shrewd look as we walked (achingly slowly!) towards the gate. 'If I didn't know better I should say you was running away from someone. Has Matron given you the say-so to leave? She usually comes out with a person what's going.'

And then the worst happened. Before I could answer, Ralph let out a loud wail from somewhere deep in my coat. He must have had enough of being bumped up and down like a sack of potatoes, and decided at last it was time to make his feelings known.

The porter and I stared at each other for what seemed a very long time. Then the old man tugged at the top of my coat to reveal the baby's red, cross face, bobbing about against my chest as he cried.

'Please don't say anything,' I begged the porter, trying to comfort Ralph at the same time. 'I've not taken any workhouse property, only this little mite, and my sister asked me to. I shall take good care of him. Please let us go!'

He scratched one of the sideburns thoughtfully, whilst I nearly burst out of my skin with impatience. We had to get out before the matron came running! And then at last he said, 'Ach, be off with you. One bastard child more or less in this place won't make much difference.' And he opened the gate to let me out.

We had escaped! But what *was* I going to do with Iris's baby now?

FOURTEEN

Girls if taken from the workhouse school at thirteen or fourteen with previous good character, and trained for half-a-year in a lady's house or a cottager's, can be turned into very nice, good servants. But before sent off to service they should be under special, kind, loving care and interest, so their heart and mind is touched and, as it were, opened to good influence.

From *Our Servants – Their Duties to Us, and Ours to Them*, Mrs Eliot James, 1882

I did not get back to the Hall until after midnight, having tramped all the way from Edenvale station in the bitter cold. Our bedroom was empty, although I had thought someone would have been tucked up there asleep by now, since Megan and Becky were meant to have had the afternoon off. I unlaced my boots and lay down on the bed as I was, too weary even to think of undressing. Just as I was closing my eyes, Megan came into the room, wearing her black uniform and cap.

'Oh, there you are,' she said at the sight of me. 'And how's your poor mother? Any better, is she?'

I had thought it safer not to tell anyone where I had been really going that day. Luckily Megan did not wait for a reply, but sat down on her own bed with a thump and kicked off her shoes. 'Lord, there's tired I am! My hair will have to look after itself tonight.'

I had never seen Megan go to sleep without first putting in her rag rollers; she must have been worn out. 'I thought you had the afternoon off?' I asked, already feeling guilty that I had not been there to do my part.

She yawned. 'There was a telegram, see, to say the Brookfields are back early. Staying in London tonight, and then down to Swallowcliffe in the morning. Mrs Henderson don't know what to do with herself. Running around chasing her tail, she is.'

'Let's hope she's made up her mind and Master Edward will be put out of his misery,' Becky said, coming in with Jane. 'She must know whether she wants to marry him by now, surely.'

'I'll bet she's met somebody else in Italy,' Jane said. She took off her cap and began unpinning her hair. 'A beautiful young lady like that, with all her money. Then we shall be in trouble – Thomas thinks half of us will lose our jobs in the new year, the way things are going. That means you and Megan will be out, Polly. Junior maids are always the first.'

I grunted; Megan said nothing, having already fallen asleep.

'Now don't go worrying the poor girl,' Becky said, slipping out of her dress. 'You'll just have to persuade Miss Brookfield to marry Master Edward, Polly. She's taken quite a shine to you, hasn't she? Although I still think she'd be better off with Master Rory.'

The very sound of Rory Vye's name made my blood boil, after what I had been through that day. He must have been Ralph's father: the baby had his blue eyes and, now I came to think about it, the same dimple on his tiny chin. What was it Iris had said? The boy's father had been 'not such a fine gentleman after all'. Well, that was true enough. To have given her money to get rid of the child, as if that was all he needed to do! Miss Brookfield would have nothing to do with Master Rory if I could possibly help it.

Tired though I was, sleep took a long time coming that night. I could not stop thinking about Ralph, and wondering whether I had done right by him. He had started crying in earnest as we ran out of the workhouse and back along Union Street; I guessed he must have been hungry. Only when we had reached the end of the road and turned a corner did I think it safe to stop and try to hush him.

'Are you not going to feed the poor little thing?' came a voice from somewhere near by, and I looked up to see a woman watching me from the doorway of a nearby terraced house, her arms folded.

'This is my sister's baby,' I said, patting Ralph on the back and rocking him about in the way my brother and sisters used to like when they were small. 'I've no milk to give him.'

The woman clicked her tongue, clearly not thinking a great deal of me or my sister. 'Try Mrs Clare's place,' she said. 'Mebbe ten doors away? Number sixty-one. She's had one of her own not long since.' She went back inside and slammed the door.

I did not know what Iris would think about a stranger nursing her baby, but beggars can't be choosers. Mrs Clare came to the door with a swarm of young children around her feet – some of them without shoes, I noticed, despite the cold – and said she would feed Ralph for a sixpence.

'I have no money left, ma'am,' I told her, 'but I can scrub your floor and put the kettle on for a drop o' tea whilst you sit down.'

'And what makes you think my floor will need scrubbing?' she said, drawing herself up in a huff. When I told her I had only suggested it having nothing else to offer, however, she warmed up a little and told me to come in.

My mother would have died before she'd let her kitchen get in that state! There must have been a week's worth of dirt, dust and vegetable peelings on the floor, and the table needed scrubbing too, though I made do with a wipe. Mrs Clare sat herself down and watched me work while Ralph guzzled away at her breast as though he were starving – which, come to think of it, he probably was. At least she made a better wet-nurse than a housewife.

'You're a good worker, I'll say that,' she said when I had done my best in the kitchen. 'If you have a go at the front step as well, you can have some more of my milk to take away with you. None of mine likes the bottle, but this little fellow won't be so particular, I reckon.'

Ralph slept all the way to the railway station. The rhythm of my footsteps helped clear my head, and by the time our train arrived, I had come up with a plan. There was no telling whether it would work, but at least it was worth a try. Instead of taking the train straight back to Edenvale, I got out at Little Rising and sat in the station for an hour or so until it was dark. You might be thinking I had changed my mind about going to my mother, but I knew she would never agree to look after Ralph. How many times had she told me all the work there was in bringing up a baby, besides the expense, and the heartache?

Not to mention the fact that this child had no father to speak of, and everyone was bound to think it was mine. No, I had decided upon making my way to another house in the village – but not until it was dark, in case I came across someone I knew who might recognise me. This visit would be better kept secret.

Mrs Chadwick herself came to the door of the Rectory when I rang on the bell. She was all alone in the house; the Reverend must have been taking Evensong and there was no maid about. When I reminded her who I was, she took me into the kitchen and listened while I talked without saying a word. I did not tell her everything, only what she needed to know: that here was a baby of a month old, whose mother was not in a position to look after him and whose father did not know he existed. He was in desperate need of a loving home, and I could think of no better place than this to bring him. Then I put Ralph in her arms and gave her the bottle of Mrs Clare's milk to feed him with. He had woken up by now and was beginning to grizzle.

'I shall have to talk to my husband,' Mrs Chadwick said. 'It is quite an undertaking, to bring up someone else's child. What if the mother wants him back one day? And what sort of woman is she, anyway?'

I took the photograph of Iris out of my coat pocket and showed it to her. 'She is an honest, decent person, even though she might have taken a wrong turning in life. I don't think she will ever be in a position to care properly for her son, but she loves him very much and wants only the best for him. That is why she gave him up, and it nearly killed her to do it. Will you take him in, out of Christian charity? You can see what a dear little thing he is.'

We both looked at the baby. He had stopped sucking on the bottle for a moment and was gazing up at Mrs Chadwick's homely face with such an expression of wonder, she couldn't help smiling down at him. I knew there and then that he had stolen her heart; the decision was made, no matter what Reverend Chadwick might have to say about it. All that remained was to tell her the baby's name (I felt we should let Iris decide about that – it was the least she deserved, even if the name was a little too close to the boy's father's for my liking), give her the locket and photograph, and ask whether I might come and visit the child from time to time – without my mother's knowledge, if possible. Somehow, I did not want her knowing that it was Iris's baby who had come to the village.

'Leave me your address,' Mrs Chadwick said, as I was about to leave. 'We shall write to you about him. Discreetly, of course.' Perhaps she thought Ralph was my own son, despite what I had told her.

Although I had done the best I could, I felt very much alone as I walked back to the station. I missed Ralph's warm body snuggled against mine, the smell of him, and the little snuffling noises he made while dropping off to sleep. My heart went out to Iris. She had lost her child: the pain of that must have been a thousand times sharper than anything I felt. How could she bear it?

I thought about Iris a great deal over the next few days, what with Christmas coming up and all those carols about the birth of the Christ child. Mr Wilkins taught us a new one called 'Away in a Manger', which had something about the 'little lord Jesus laying down his sweet head'. Every time we came to that line, it made me think of Ralph on his straw mattress in the workhouse, and I was hard pressed not to burst out crying. The Hall seemed so merry and bright – decorated with red-berried holly, evergreen branches and a great fir tree lit up with candles – and everyone in such fine spirits, looking forward to the wonderful dinner we would have in the servants' hall on Christmas Day, and the fun and games afterwards. Of course I was pleased to see Miss Brookfield again, and hoped with all my heart that she would decide to marry Master Edward, but I couldn't take pleasure in anything; not now I knew the state Iris was in, only a few miles away.

On Christmas Eve I received a card in the post from the Reverend and Mrs Chadwick, wishing me the compliments of the season and encouraging me in my Bible study

— Luke's Gospel, chapter two, verse forty, would be particularly helpful. I looked it up and read, 'And the child grew, and waxed strong in spirit, filled with wisdom: and the grace of God was upon him.' That was a relief (and fancy Mrs Chadwick dreaming up such a clever way to let me know), but it made me sorry that I could not tell Iris her son was safely settled, with good people looking after him. It was dreadful to think of her, shut up in the workhouse all alone and desperate for news. And yet how could I go back there? Matron would have me up before the magistrate for kidnapping, soon as winking.

Later that evening, the table in the servants' hall was piled high with presents which Lady Vye gave out to each person; we maids had a length of printed cotton each to make new work dresses, while the menservants were presented with starched collars. Afterwards, the rest of the family and their guests came through to listen to us sing. We ran through all the old favourites such as 'Good King Wenceslas', 'God Rest Ye, Merry Gentlemen', 'The Holly and the Ivy' and then Megan started 'Silent Night' on her own, without the piano or anything. It might have been her beautiful voice, ringing out clear as crystal, or the picture of a mother and child in the first verse, but that carol undid me completely. By the time everyone else had joined in, the tears I had held back for so long came bursting out and I had to slip away before making a spectacle of myself.

As I stumbled along the corridor with my apron pressed to my eyes, I heard a voice calling after me. Then I found myself being steered through a door and into a chair; I was in Mrs Henderson's room, and she was sitting opposite me.

'I am so sorry, ma'am,' I hiccuped, trying to control my sobs. 'I don't know what came over me. I shall be all right in a minute.'

She gave me a few minutes to control myself. 'I had my doubts about you to begin with, Polly, as you know,' she said, and I glanced up to see her looking at me thoughtfully. 'But you have done well here. You are a hard worker and not some silly, flighty creature like a lot of them. I should like to see you staying on at Swallowcliffe and making something of yourself.'

'Thank you, ma'am,' I said, more than a little surprised.

'So you mustn't go getting any daft ideas in your head. The family go their way and we go ours, and that's all there is to it. There is no point in complaining, or weeping and wailing about the unfairness of it all. I know very well why you're in a pother, and let's not have any more claptrap about your sick mother.'

She gave me a grim smile. 'Shut your mouth or you'll be catching flies in it. There's not a lot goes on in this house that gets past me, or outside it for that matter. I know where your friend Iris ended up, more's the pity, and no doubt that was where you went the other Sunday.'

I could hardly believe what she was saying. We had been told that anyone so much as mentioning Iris's name would be dismissed, and yet here was Mrs Henderson talking about my visit to her in one breath and my future at the Hall in another. It didn't make sense! 'How did you know Iris was in the workhouse?' I asked. There was no point in pretending otherwise.

'I know the matron of old, so I asked her to let me know if an Iris Baker turned up there. A good few maids have come to Swallowcliffe from Hardingbridge workhouse over the years, although not many have done as well for themselves as Jemima Newgate. There, I've surprised you again, haven't I? Anyway, that is beside the point.' She leaned forward. 'Just because Miss Harriet fancies a chat with you every now and then, or Miss Brookfield likes the way you brush her hair, it doesn't mean you will ever be more to them than a servant – not that there is any shame in that, mind. Forget your place and you will end up in trouble. You learn from poor Iris's example.'

'But it is so unfair!' I said. 'Why is she the one to be punished, and – and—' Mrs Henderson was being very open with me, but I still could not bring myself to finish the sentence.

'And the other party gets off scot-free?' She finished it for me. 'That's the way of the world, my girl, and always will be. You might as well try to stop it turning as expect to change that – especially when there's a gentleman involved. Iris knew the rules and she broke them anyway. Not so sharp then, was I? By the time I found out, it was too late, and I shall always be sorry for that.' She stood up. 'Now, dry your eyes and think carefully about what I have said. I'll not make a habit of talking like this, and I trust you won't go yattering to the others about it.'

'No, ma'am,' I said. 'Only, there is one last thing. Do you think the matron would let me see Iris again?'

Now it was Mrs Henderson's turn to look surprised. 'But don't you know? I thought that's what this crying was all about. I am afraid none of us will be seeing Iris again – not in this lifetime, anyway. She passed away last week.'

FIFTEEN

It sometimes happens among the poorer classes that the female relatives attend the funeral; but this custom is by no means to be recommended, since in these cases it but too frequently happens that, being unable to restrain their emotions, they interrupt and destroy the solemnity of the ceremony with their sobs, and even by fainting.

From *Cassell's Household Guide*, c. 1880s

The matron had written to Mrs Henderson again, informing her that both Iris and the baby had now left their earthly troubles behind. I suppose she did not care to admit that the child had been smuggled out of the workhouse and was still alive somewhere, perhaps causing trouble because of his very existence, instead of having the decency to set everyone's mind at rest by dying quietly with his mother. The money that Iris had been keeping for the baby's future had been used to cover their funeral expenses, she said, since the girl's family was unwilling to contribute; they had been buried together in unconsecrated ground at the side of the Hardingbridge churchyard. I was too shocked by the news to tell Mrs Henderson where Iris's baby really was, which was probably just as well since it would surely only have got me in all sorts of difficulties.

'All this must remain strictly between the two of us,' she said. 'There is no point in upsetting the others when we've so much work to get through. I have taken you into my confidence, Polly – don't let me down. Now, get along with you.'

I couldn't think what to do with myself. There was a little while to spare before we needed to go about our duties upstairs, so I ended up huddled on the floor in a corner of the china room. It was peaceful and dark, with the sound of the carol-singing drifting only faintly through the door as I sat there with my back against the cupboard door. Iris was gone. My dear, sweet friend had died in that godforsaken place, with no one to comfort her. She must have known how ill she was: that was why she had asked me to come and take Ralph away. And then, without him, she had lost the will to live. It was hardly to be borne.

At last I wiped my face and walked slowly back to the servants' hall. The family and their guests had begun filing out, already in pairs, for their procession into dinner. I flattened myself against the doorway of the china room as they went past. There was Miss Brookfield in her jewels and lovely evening gown on Master Edward's arm, and there was Master Rory, following behind with another young lady who was smiling up at him as he told her some amusing story. How I hated him, with his easy, meaningless charm! It seemed extraordinary to me that he could walk by without feeling the heat of my stare as I stood in the shadows, watching him. Yet he did, and so did the rest of the party, and no one even noticed I was there.

And what if one of them *had* seen me, and even happened to glance at my face? 'She has probably had some squabble with one of the parlourmaids,' this person might have thought, if it had occurred to him or her to think anything at all, 'or perhaps the housekeeper has had reason to speak sharply to her, or someone left a smaller tip than she was expecting. That is the trouble with servants these days. They are never satisfied!'

I was very bitter, which you will no doubt understand and forgive. My grief lay like a cold, heavy stone in the middle of my chest, dragging me down. I nursed it to myself for the rest of that night and the next day too – which was Christmas, and hardly a time for such sad thoughts. We went to church and had turkey and plum pudding in the servants' hall for dinner, and played snapdragon afterwards, snatching raisins with our teeth out of a bowlful of burning brandy, and then watched the wide-eyed tenants' children receiving their presents – and all I could think about the whole time was Iris.

'Just you stop worrying about that mammy of yours,' Megan said, when we were filling up the hip baths that evening. 'Since when did moping around with a long face ever help anybody?' But that only made me feel guilty about the lies I had told.

I went over and over in my mind everything that Mrs Henderson had said, and what she had chosen not to say. Why hadn't she punished me for going to see Iris? Why had she taken such trouble to explain her thoughts to me? The only answer I could come up with was that she must have been fond of Iris, in her way. Although she had had no choice but to dismiss her, she might have felt sorry for her. She would not have gone so far as to visit Iris herself, but she had chosen not to stand in my way. Perhaps she was a little fond of me, too, and did not want to see me making the same mistake.

And then, suddenly, I remembered the extraordinary fact that Jemima had come to Swallowcliffe from the workhouse. To think of her growing up in a place like that! She was not a cut above the rest of us after all, not by any stretch of the imagination. Perhaps that was why she had wanted my locket: not for the thing itself, but for my mother's love that came with it. If I had clawed my way up through the workhouse, who's to say I'd have turned out any better than Jemima? All the things I thought I knew about the world seemed to be shifting; the only fact for certain being that it was a strange and confusing place.

On Boxing Day, Miss Brookfield had the chance to fulfil her promise to Harriet. The local hunt was meeting in the village, and the whole family and their guests were taking part – with the exception of little John and Mrs Brookfield, who would be going by carriage to see the riders and hounds set off and then returning to Swallowcliffe. Mrs Brookfield would be going back to America in a few days, and still nobody knew whether her daughter would be going with her.

'She won't marry him,' Becky said. 'She would have said yes by now, surely.'

I thought there was still hope, but the signs didn't look promising.

We servants watched the party assemble in the courtyard. They did look fine, particularly Lady Vye and Miss Brookfield in their tightly-fitting habits, white stocks tied high under the chin, and dashing top hats. Both of them so graceful on horseback, too. I had heard that clearing fences was twice as hard in a side-saddle, and hoped my young lady would be careful. She was mounted on a large grey horse which was stamping its hooves and blowing down its nose in a very flighty-looking manner. At least Miss Harriet should be safe on old Snowdrop, who looked a very placid creature, even though she was always complaining he was too slow. And there was Master Rory having a tussle with his great black hunter; I hoped it would throw him off and stamp on him too, for good measure. The brute had taken a crafty sideways kick at the wiry brown mare his brother was riding. Anyone could see Master Edward was not as confident in the saddle as the others and the mare seemed to sense it as well: she kept stretching out her neck and clanking on the bit with her big yellow teeth. (I have never been much of a one for horses, as you can probably tell.)

Thomas and William took round silver trays clinking with glasses of sherry, and then after this stirrup cup, the party moved off at last. They would be out for a good while, so we had been told we could have a couple of hours to ourselves that afternoon since it was the festive season and we would be up late again in the evening. After our dinner at midday, I fetched my shawl and coat from the back of our attic room door and stole away by myself, not being in much of a mood for company and hoping a walk to one of my favourite places might settle my thoughts. About a mile away from the Hall was a tall, narrow archway at the top of an avenue of oak trees running up the hill. This was the Fairview Tower, which had been designed by the first Lord Vye so that he could survey his land from the flat roof. It looked such a mysterious, magical building from the house, catching the last rays of the evening sun. In the summer, I had discovered the path which led up to the tower and I loved to sit on the bench at its foot, looking down at the Hall laid out like a doll's house below.

Today, however, I could take no pleasure in anything and stared at the bleak, wintry landscape with an equally frosty heart. I was not even sure whether I wanted to carry on working at Swallowcliffe – perhaps it was time to start looking for another position. I could see Iris everywhere and it was too painful. So many things reminded me of her, down to the jam jars lining the still room dresser with their labels in her neat handwriting. There was that spot on the roof where she had stood looking out into the dark. Had she any idea then where she might end up? I had a feeling she did. And yet she would not get rid of her baby just to make life easier for Rory Vye.

I don't know how long I must have sat there, gazing at the house. After a while, I realised that the sight of it was comforting, somehow. My small hopes and fears did not add up to so very much in the scheme of things. When we were all of us dead and gone, Swallowcliffe would still be standing there, peaceful as ever, while another set of people played out the story of their lives. I loved the place, as dearly as you might love a person. Where else would I want to go? Iris would always be with me – she was locked in my heart – and the fact that we had known each other here was a reason to stay, not to leave. I felt calm and quiet, and then I had a bit of a cry, and that made me feel quieter still. Empty, almost.

Then, all of a sudden, whom should I see walking up the hill towards me but William. 'So this is one of your favourite spots too,' he said, a little out of breath. 'I usually have it to myself. Do you mind if I join you?'

'Not at all,' I said, despite feeling shy and awkward that we should be sitting there alone. Still, we had come together by chance; it was not as though we had arranged to meet. Although surely William must have seen me, setting off up the hill ahead of him?

We gazed down on the house. 'It is almost a year now since you first came to Swallowcliffe,' he said, breaking the silence. 'Do you remember when I found you wandering along the corridor, in a proper temper with Mrs Bragg?'

I smiled sadly. 'It seems a very long time ago. Things have changed a great deal since then, and I have changed with them.'

'Not too much, I hope,' he said. 'Will you not tell me what is the matter, Polly? Something has upset you, I can see that. In fact, you have not been yourself for days.'

I shook my head, not sure whether I could trust myself to speak.

'Here is my handkerchief,' he said, offering it to me. 'And it happens to be the very same one I lent you twelve months ago! It has been to the laundry since then, you will be glad to hear.'

He could always manage to make me laugh, although this time again the tears were not far away. And after I had swallowed the lump in my throat and wiped my eyes, I did share with him the reason for my sadness – bearing Mrs Henderson's warning in mind but knowing that the confidence would go no further. I felt it was right to tell him what had become of Iris, since he had been so fond of her. I did not mention the baby and he did not ask about that.

'It is too bad to think of Iris in the workhouse,' he said. 'She was always clean and neat, and never so much as a spoon out of place in the still room. Well, I am very sorry for the poor girl. No wonder you are so sad.'

'And you will be too,' I said. 'I know she was your particular – I mean, I know you thought very highly of her, as she did of you.'

'Iris did not trouble herself over-much on my account,' he said. 'And she was not my particular, if you want to call it that.'

'Oh, I am sorry,' I stammered, feeling foolish. 'I thought

– well, it does not matter now what I thought.'

We stared down at the valley for another little while. And then William turned to me and said, 'I do have a particular, although it was never Iris.'

'Oh,' I said, not quite sure why he should be looking at me in that intent way. Since the question was clearly expected, I asked, 'Who *is* your particular, then?'

'Why, it is you, of course,' he replied, with a smile that would melt stone. 'Surely you must know that? From the first moment I saw you, marching down the corridor in that extraordinary dress with your eyes spitting fire and your cheeks all rosy and your hair falling out of its pins. That is the girl for me, I thought, and I have not had reason to change my mind since then. So, what do you have to say about that, Miss Perkins?'

I had absolutely no idea. 'But I am only fifteen,' I said. It was the first thing that came into my head.

'I know. And I am eighteen. That is not such a great difference.'

'I do not want to leave Swallowcliffe – not for a while, at least.' Oh dear. Surely I could come up with a better remark than that!

'Neither do I. All I am thinking is that perhaps we might happen to meet up here or in some other quiet place now and then, and pass the time of day. Come the summer, I might even walk over to your village from mine and pay my respects to your family. Do you think that would be all right?'

'Yes,' I said, 'I think it would be perfectly fine. In fact, I should like it very much.'

'Good. Then that's settled.' If only he would stop smiling at me like that! No wonder I could hardly think straight.

We might have said all sorts of other things then, but suddenly William stared down at the valley. 'Look!' he said, taking my arm. 'That is very strange.'

A man on horseback was riding towards the house – not in a roundabout, coming-home-tired-from-the-hunting sort of way, but galloping hell for leather. 'That is Master Rory, I think,' William said, narrowing his eyes at the distant figure. 'I hope nothing is wrong.'

It was time we were getting back anyway, so I sent William down the hill first, waited five minutes and then ran along the path myself. Please God let Harriet and Miss Brookfield be all right, I prayed – which was dreadful of me, I know. About halfway back to the Hall, I saw a carriage tearing down the drive, with Master Rory sitting up beside the coachman. That whirling feeling in the pit of my stomach grew stronger.

'There you are!' Mary said, as soon as she caught sight of me. 'Quickly, make up the fire in Master Edward's room. And take these extra sheets and towels with you.

Megan is already up there.' She thrust a pile of clean linen into my arms.

'What is it?' I asked her. 'Whatever has happened?'

'Ask me no questions and I'll tell you no lies. Just hurry along and do as I say.'

She might as well have told me straight out what was the matter, since we all found out soon enough anyway, but there you are. It turned out that there *had* been an accident, and a bad one too: Master Edward's horse had thrown him at a hedge and then rolled over on top of him. They brought him back on a stretcher and took him up to his bedroom.

'How bad is he, do you think?' Megan whispered to me as we went back downstairs. All we could find out was that he was still unconscious, and it remained to be seen when – or if – he would come round. Luckily, the doctor was a keen huntsman and not more than five minutes away on his own horse, which was a blessing. We had done everything we could to help Master Edward; now God would have to take care of the rest. Lord and Lady Vye were at his bedside, and so was his brother Rory. It had been thought too upsetting an experience for Harriet, although I knew she would have wanted to be there, especially with her medical ambitions.

I tapped on Miss Brookfield's door later that evening to see if she needed anything. Lady Vye had told Mrs Bragg that dinner was not to be served downstairs, but that her guests might like a light supper on a tray in their rooms. There was no reply, so I opened the door a little way. Miss Brookfield was sitting staring into the distance. She did not notice me come in, and I had to ask her twice whether she wanted anything to eat before she could think what to reply.

'Don't worry, Miss,' I told her, seeing she was in need of some comfort and apparently no one to give it but me. 'He will be all right, you'll see. The Vyes are a tough old breed – that's why the family's lasted for all these years.'

'But what if he isn't? You don't understand!' She buried her face in her hands. 'This is all my fault! If Edward dies, it is down to me.'

'How can that be, Miss?' I asked, thinking she had taken leave of her senses. 'You couldn't make an accident happen.'

'We were riding along together, the three of us,' she said. 'Rory jumped the hedge first and I followed. It was high, but my horse wanted to take it and I let him have his head. Why didn't I think? I should have known the jump was too much for Edward, and that he would have died rather than admit it. Well, now he might – die, that is. If I had turned back, this would never have happened.'

'But you said so yourself: it was Master Rory who went over the hedge first, not you. If anyone has to take the blame, it should be him.'

'I shouldn't have followed Rory,' she whispered. 'Edward was bound to come after us. I knew those boys had some silly competition over me and I should have put a stop to it well before now.'

'Master Edward and Master Rory have been rivals from the moment Rory was born,' I told her, repeating something I had heard Mrs Henderson say. 'They are always fighting over something, and perhaps this time it was you. But that makes this accident no more your fault than it was the fault of the fat brown trout that Rory fell in the lake, trying to land him before Edward could.'

She laughed.

'I'll tell you something else,' I said, 'if you'll forgive my impertinence. Be careful of Rory Vye, Miss. He will break your heart and not think twice about it.'

She stared at me for a long moment. 'Whatever makes you say that?'

'Because I have seen the damage he has caused,' I said. 'He destroyed somebody who was very dear to me, and I could not bear to let him hurt you too. Follow your head this time, Miss Brookfield.'

There, I had done it now. But if I had not told her what I thought of Master Rory, I should never have forgiven myself.

*

Six months have passed since Edward's accident. It is a warm day in June, and we are gathered in a semi-circle around the front entrance at Swallowcliffe. 'Lovely day for a wedding,' somebody mutters for the hundredth time, gazing up at the bright blue sky. We are waiting for the bride to come out and climb into the barouche that will take her to the village church, where her groom and guests are waiting. The carriage has been garlanded with roses and orange blossom, and the four grey horses have had their manes plaited and tied with white ribbons. There are flowers in every room of the Hall, because the wedding breakfast will take place here after the service. At first they wanted to hold the ceremony in our little chapel, but it was nowhere near big enough for so many guests. We shall be more than twenty in the house over the next few days, and a noisy lot those Americans are too.

'Here she is,' Megan whispers, clutching my arm. 'Oh, there's beautiful!'

I had not been able to help Miss Brookfield dress this morning; now that she is almost a grand married lady, a proper maid has been found for her from Paris. 'She is rather stiff and starchy,' Miss Brookfield whispered to me when I brought up her hot water last night, 'but maybe we shall get used to each other in time. If only you were a few years older, Polly! But Lady Vye said I could not possibly go on having a maid of fifteen.'

211

'Sixteen now, Miss,' I said, as if that made any difference.

'To think this is the last night I shall go to bed as Kate Brookfield,' she said, sighing. 'Well, I hope I am doing the right thing.'

I can just make out her face through the cloudy veil as she walks past on her father's arm, looking very solemn and serious. William opens the door of the barouche and up she climbs, the French maid holding the long train of her dress so that it won't tear and then arranging it carefully around her feet. She waves to us and we all wave back, and then somebody cheers, which Mr Goddard looks a bit cross about at first, but before long everyone is cheering and clapping and he has joined in just as heartily as the rest. There can't be a single person here who isn't delighted Miss Brookfield is marrying our Master Edward, especially after everything he has been through, and what could be wrong with showing it?

It took him a long time to get over that accident. For two weeks we did not know which way the dice would fall. Apparently, the horse had done a great deal of damage when it rolled on top of him – which stands to reason, I suppose, a great heavy animal like that. And then slowly, he began to get better. There had to be a nurse with him most of the time and the family took turns sitting at his bedside too, Miss Brookfield included. She would not go back to America until she knew he was on the mend, and somehow the date for her return kept slipping further and further back. At last, her mother went home without her, and we had a good idea then how the land lay. She and Master Edward had spent a great deal of time together, and Master Rory had eventually been told to rejoin his regiment so he was not around to complicate matters. I am sure he did not want to go and leave Miss Brookfield alone with his brother, but there was nothing much he could do. Serve him right! That's what I thought. Let him see for once what it's like to want something and not have it, just like the rest of us. He is the only one not to look happy this morning, but I cannot find it in my heart to feel any sympathy at the sight of his miserable face. I am glad to think of him in pain, after all the suffering he has caused others.

William and Thomas climb up beside the coachman and the carriage pulls away. I know William would dearly like to wink at me but of course he cannot in front of all these people. How fine he looks this morning! I don't know why he should be so fond of me, but I am very glad that he is. We are better friends than ever and, although we have to be careful about being seen together at the Hall, he is to come and visit me when I am home at Little Rising for my week's holiday later in the summer. I plan to call in at the Rectory and see how young Ralph is doing. My mother wrote to tell me that the Chadwicks had taken in a foundling baby, and you never saw such a beautiful child. He is the apple of their eye, apparently, and not yet been heard to cry.

Iris would be so proud of her boy; I hope that somewhere she's looking down on him and knows he is happy. I shall watch over Ralph for the rest of my life and help him in any way I can, for her sake. Who knows? Maybe one day I might even shame Rory Vye into providing for his son. That would be worth the wait.